MATED TO THE PACK

A REVERSE HAREM PARANORMAL ROMANCE

JADE ALTERS

VIVIAN

"Señorita Vivian," our local guide, Fernando, said in his thick Spanish accent. "You have mail."

The deeply tanned Colombian handed me a manila envelope, and I winced. The address on the piece of mail was grandma's family lawyer and probably had papers about Nona's estate. No one had contacted me when she fell at home; the neighbors found her and got her to the hospital. I was hard to track, en route from Colorado to Colombia for this dig, and she passed before they could reach me. I felt like hell that I wasn't there for her final hours.

Nona dying sent me into an emotional maelstrom on what should have been a coup for my academic career. Professor Robbins picked me to assist him on the dig even though I had completed only one semester of my two-year program. He even pulled out a scholarship somewhere to cover my costs.

"And here is your backpack, Señorita. You forgot it again." Fernando handed me the battered green-gray thing.

When I went to look for it before I left, I couldn't find it. And since the last bus to the hotel was leaving, I had to hope it would turn up. On my first day, Rick urged me to leave my valuables in the hotel safe.

There was nothing consequential in it, except my notebook, a few sundries to spare me the worst effects of the dry mountain air and a couple of small finds that I meant to catalogue. I think of them with guilt because I shouldn't have them there.

"You can't keep an eye on everything," he had said. "And while most of the locals we hire to help us are good people, there is always someone who thinks any American is rich and can afford to replace possessions."

"Thanks, Fernando. My grandmother always said I'd lose my head if it wasn't attached."

"We don't want you to lose such a pretty head."

"Now, now, Fernando. We talked about this. No flirting."

He smiled widely at me, his white teeth in contrast with his brown skin. Fernando wasn't my type, being in his forties and married with five children, but that didn't stop him from saying the odd inappropriate then.

"Okay, Señorita, business talk only. So where do we go today, Señorita Blake?"

"I guess we'll go back to our first dig," I spoke as I jammed the envelope into my backpack. Professor Robbins convinced the people funding this dig that more untouched graves existed here, despite the centuries of grave robbers that pilfered the riches of those ancient people. The base camp location we set up in sat in the Rocky Mountains near San Augustine, nearby the treasure trove of antiquities preserved in the national park for that purpose. My favorite was the fantastic stone totems of human faces with canine fangs that grinned with eerie friendliness. There was something about those faces, all too human yet alien; it fascinated me.

Fernando clucked his disapproval of my plan. "I am not

sure that is a good idea, Señorita Blake. The LI are crawling all over that area right now."

I huffed. The Los Ignas was one of Colombia's most notorious, dangerous, and deadly guerrilla forces. Their crimes ranged from stealing children to serve in their army to drug running. Their connections with powerful drug lords subjected them to severe government retribution, promoting an endless cycle of violence between the government and the LI. Fernando reminded me that their presence was dangerous—all I could think was how damned inconvenient it was to work around them.

A spray of automatic gunfire rattled through the rocky terrain. A month into my dig, the distant rat-tat-tat no longer alarmed me—the weapon's fire that drew closer did. Dirt flew before a jeep careened down the road toward the base camp. Fernando threw me to the ground behind a rough wooden bench out the base tent. The hard jolt shuddered through my body, but I turned to my back to see what happened. To my horror Fernando fell to the ground with a gunshot wound to the head.

"Fernando!" I yelled. Another round of rifle fire came so close I had to cover my ears with my hands; the deafening sound swallowed my scream. My heart's rapid beating rattled in my ears.

I peeked over the upturned bench to watch a jeep slide to an abrupt halt next to me. One man drove, and another crouched in the flatbed of the battered vehicle. Another spray of automatic fire flew from the rifle in his hand, upending another jeep. It's occupants flew out while it overturned with its wheels spinning.

One of the tallest men I've ever seen stood in the bed of the jeep. He wore camos, a matching wide-brimmed hat and sunglasses. His square-cut jaw sported a two-day old growth of dark stubble. He leaped out of the vehicle and with his massive arms reached down and hauled me to my feet.

"Get in."

"I'm not going anywhere with you," I said defiantly. I tried to squirm, but the man held me by my neck as firmly as a mother dog held her pups by the scruff of the neck. His nostrils flared as he clutched me, and he turned his head away for a second.

"Don't be foolish. Rick sent us to get you out of here," he said in a gravelly voice.

"Where's Rick?"

"Not in a good place. But the sooner you get in that jeep, the sooner I can go and retrieve him."

"It's the LI, isn't it?"

"Climb in!" he snarled. "Or I'll throw you in."

"My things! Our research!"

He shook his head. "Choose. Your shit or your life. Pick now, because I don't have time for this."

I slung my backpack over my back and climbed into the beat-up transport while my gut did somersaults. My head burst with questions: Who were these men? Where was Rick? What the hell had happened?

"The airstrip, Boss?" the driver asked.

"Yes, and don't call me Boss."

"Yes, Sir!" said the driver enthusiastically, which earned another scowl. Seriously, did this man not smile? Then the driver's words connected with my brain.

"Airstrip?" I squeaked. "I don't have my passport."

The big man cocked his head. "That's the least of your problems. Sparks, bug-out!"

The driver jammed his foot on the accelerator, and I flew back into the seat with a grunt. This guy wasn't as big as 'Boss,' and he wore sunglasses, and a green baseball cap along with the green and brown camos that mirrored what Boss wore. Which military claimed these guys?

"Who are you?" I screamed over the roar of the wind whipping in my ears, the whine of the engine and a rattling sound from within the body of the vehicle. But the driver sped along the deeply rutted road without glancing at me, and I struggled to keep my seat as the rocky terrain whipped by in a blur.

Maybe he didn't hear me. The man kept deadly serious attention to the road and his driving as the road dipped, rose and curved. Gears ground as he worked his muscular arm to counter the dangerous conditions of the road.

My stomach lurched and rolled as if I were sea-sick and urged me to retch, but I didn't dare ask him to stop. We were on the run for our lives and the people that had chased them —and possibly captured Rick—took no prisoners.

Where were we going, what was going to happen to us, and what was my professor's fate? This driver must know something, but he's too busy driving, and I didn't know if I was fleeing from danger or walking into it.

We twisted off the road at some signal I didn't catch, and our path jerking up the hillside made the thoroughfare we left seem like a superhighway. I gripped my seat so tightly I lost sensation in my fingers. We took a flying leap at the edge and landed, racing full speed toward a prop plane sitting at one end of the plateau. My heart almost ripped open my rib cage trying to escape.

We skidded to a halt within ten feet of the plane and a man wearing a headset leaned out.

"Where's the rest?"

"The primary got delayed."

"I can't wait."

"I know. Take her —" He swung his head toward me. His nose crinkled as if he whiffed something bad. Wow. I took a shower this morning. Did I smell rank so soon? "Where do you live?"

"I go to school in Colorado."

"Dude!" called the man.

"Where else? Where is the safest place for you? A friend? A relative?"

I shrugged my shoulders.

"Connecticut. My grandma's house is there."

"Get her to Connecticut."

"Not the flight path I filed," complained the pilot. "Documents?"

"Lost in transit."

"Complications," the man said with a frown.

"You know where to send the bill," growled Boss.

"Your dime, not mine." The man beckoned to me with his hand.

"Hop on, Miss," said the pilot. "Thank you for choosing Air Karmon."

LUCIUS

*D*aniel took point. I was at his six, with Kyle behind me and Sean at the rear. The army calls a four-man unit a fire team, and that was us—Fire Team Wolf. We douse figurative fires in hot spots around the globe; though since the Army cut Kyle and me, it's for the money, not serving our country.

The Army had every right to discharge us. My pack brother and I were very young when we enlisted—which was *not* an excuse. It's on us that we allowed the recruiter to hand in false birth certificates and high school transcripts. Still the word *dishonorable* sticks in my craw. Kyle and I put our lives on the line for our country, and it scores my soul that stupid teenage tricks tainted our work.

The rest of our unit, Daniel and Sean, followed us out at the end of their enlistment. Our pack bond is tighter than family. That's why I trust each man here.

This job? I've seen worse places. The area around San Agustin, Colombia was pleasant. The dew point was low, rapidly shifting cloud cover scattered the sun, and the odor of tropical orchids hung in the air. A lush canopy of gleaming leaves created a roof over our heads, and giant palm fronds fight for snatches of bright sun and sky through the canopy. Ropy vines snaked down tall trees and the dense green undergrowth sprouted across a bed of lush soil.

August is the least wet month in Colombia. Almost a paradise, except for the terrorists disguised as a people's army that infected the hills. Insects fluttered and small animals skittered. But on the job, I can't shift and take a welcome run through this rainforest.

Rick, our idiot employer got himself captured by the LI. A hotshot CIA, he acted more like a junior g-man, dragging that girl along for cover. For a reason there's no time to parse, I was ticked he did. I'd shut the book on this account after this job is done. Our work is dangerous enough without taking stupid chances with untrained assets on a mission.

We moved forward armed with our AR-15s, and I missed the weight of my usual and larger M-16. But this was a retrieval mission only, sparked by an automatic order Rick set up before he took off to Colombia for his dig. He transmitted a signal to us each night if things were good. When we didn't get it, we jumped in and located the ass by his subdermal transponder—spook gear. The extraction got more complicated when he ordered us to yank his assistant and get her on a plane.

We didn't need to babysit assets dragged along for window dressing. With reservations, I left behind Kyle and Daniel, and Sean and I retrieved the woman. Kyle and Daniel tried to scout by seeking high ground after we left, but Robbins couldn't follow because he supposedly injured his ankle—but not enough for him to make a break for it while the LI tracked my guys.

I disliked Robbins and that was an understatement, but we'd finish the mission. If we didn't, we wouldn't get paid.

Daniel halted and drew cover from a tree. He hand-signed what he spotted a thousand yards ahead. I replied that Sean needed to keep an eye out. This close, the LI would have sentries. Daniel dropped his pack and his gun, and I tried to catch his attention. This was not good place to shift.

Damn it, he does.

There are no wolves in South America which is why I told the team we would not shift here for several reasons. It's never a good idea for a local to spot a non-indigenous animal. There were advantages to our wolf form, one of them being greater stealth, but scents of prey and sudden movements distracted our animal forms.

And, the ticks are damn annoying.

Kyle moved up to Daniel's position as Daniel padded into the undergrowth. As our scout, there was no one better to recon and assess situations, but damn it, he has to listen to me. There would be an ass whooping later.

We waited until Daniel returned. He jerked his head forward, signaling the all clear. When I saw his ears pinned back, I knew he saw something he didn't like. Still, we advanced cautiously under his direction.

Daniel led us to Rick sitting against a tree. At first, I thought he'd passed, but his chest barely rose and fell, and when Daniel sniffed his face, Rick woke with a start.

"What the hell," he groaned.

"It's me, Robbins."

"Chambers," he said. "Is Vivian safe?"

"She's on her way out of the country," Sean rumbled in a growl. "I made sure of it."

I caught an edge in his voice as if he was angry. It reminded me of how I felt ticked that Robbins put that poor girl in danger.

"Good," he sighed.

"How bad?" said Kyle as he dropped Daniel's pack on the ground before he knelt by Robbins.

"Bad. After getting separated from you guys, they picked me up off the road and argued what to do with me. One wanted to kill me and the other wanted to ransom me, so they compromised and knifed me."

"That will be a story to tell your ghost friends," I snorted. *Terrorists.* I hated these informal armies because its members had no discipline.

"When I couldn't go any farther, they said they'd be back with a stretcher."

Kyle lifted Robbin's shirt and then pulled up his pack with his medical supplies.

"Okay, we'll pack it and then get you out of here."

"You can't. They'll catch up and kill you. Leave me here. They'll make sure they keep me alive to collect a ransom."

"Fuck that," I said. "We don't leave our mission behind."

"And you don't know all the things we can do," said Sean. He whipped his knife out.

"Avoid the poison ivy," said Kyle with a smirk.

"There's poison ivy here?" said Sean with consternation. The last time he ran through a patch was a source of amusement for a week.

"I guess we'll find out," said Kyle.

"Jerk," scoffed Sean. He melted into the greenery to look for suitable branches for the litter we'd construct.

"Tick-Tock," I said. "Daniel."

Daniel growled, but he pulled his pack behind Robbins, shifted, and dressed.

"I do better scouting when—"

I held up my hand and cocked my head to the human. "No time for discussion." Meaning: *We will not talk about our wolf-shifter status in front of the human.*

Daniel nodded and then joined Sean to retrieve the branches we needed. My men were well-trained—the best— and within fifteen minutes they had the litter constructed.

Kyle tended to Robbins while I kept a look-out for the LI. Either we were lucky, they were lazy, or both, because they seem to have disappeared. That was until Sean and Kyle lifted Robbins onto the stretcher, and my wolf hearing detected movement less than a click away. They would arrive in about twelve minutes, and we needed to bug out before they got here.

"Mount-up," I ordered.

Kyle and I were at the front, Sean and Daniel at the rear, so we felt no weight from Robbins.

He put his hand on my arm.

"Vivian," he gasped.

I glanced over my shoulder and spotted the red blood spreading through his gauze. He needed evac and medical care and shouldn't worry about a woman we already got to safety.

"What about her?"

"She has the intel I took, and they'll be looking for it."

"Boss," said Sean in a warning voice. I caught it too. The insurgents increasing their pace rumbled through the forest floor. My gut churned, and anger sparked again at the idea that Robbins put a woman, whose name I just learned, in danger.

"Now, Boss," warned Sean, and I made another mental note on 'coaching' him with the correct form of address.

"Protect her," croaked Robbins before he passed out.

I didn't know what I was more annoyed about: this FUBAR mission, or that Vivian was still in danger. I didn't have time to think about it.

"Forward," I barked, and our pack took off at a run.

I hopped over the back of the couch to land next to Sean who sat concentrating grim-faced on his video game blazing across the hotel wide screen.

"Hey, Sparkie."

"F.K," he grunted. Sean called me F. K. especially when he was in a bad mood.

F. K. does not stand for what people assume. Never walk around with a last name like Oberon if you want to be taken seriously by your unit. F. K. stands for Fairy King, though when one of the guys wants to yank my chain they call me Fae.

I was happy to be sitting in a hotel in Bogota, glad to get back to civilization. I never adjusted well to open landscapes despite my wolf nature, and the noisy streets of Colombia's largest town settled my nerves.

"Robbins is out of danger. Lucius hired private security to watch him in the hospital."

"Great," he grunted.

"So, we're leaving in a few hours."

"Fan-fucking-tastic," he growled.

I knocked the controller out of his hand. It sailed in a beautiful arc up, forcing Sparks to jump and grab it mid-air. He was too late, and his avatar splattered in a red haze on the virtual ground.

"Fuck," he spit.

"What's your problem?" I said.

"Asshole."

"Jerk. What's with the sour mojo?"

"None of your business." Uncharacteristically, he snapped out the words like he wanted to stab someone.

"You've been an ass since we brought Robbins in."

Sean stood and threw the controller hard into the couch. It hit so hard it bounced before settling into the cushions. My pack mate ran his hand through his hair and started pacing. Like seriously, if he kept this up he'd wear a trough in the carpet.

Sparks spun and stared at me with his hands clenched into fists at his side.

"He could have gotten her killed."

"What? That woman he brought along?"

"Yes," he hissed.

"So, what do you care? His monkey, his barrels."

"Like you understand anything, Fae," he sneered. He paced the room more furiously. His fangs grew, the hair on his hands thickened. His jaw tensed, and his lips twitched as I watched him work to keep his wolf contained. Whatever was bothering him was serious because of the four of us, Sean had been raised by humans and was the least likely to shift.

"Seriously, brah. There's a major stick up your butt."

He whirled with his face twisted in a seething rage. "Do you know where she is? Her fucking hometown. Like she is safe there. The cartel won't take long to track her."

"Did you pass that intel along to Lucius?"

"I did!" he yelled. "That's my job."

"Whoa. Chill. What's your deal?"

He scoffed and paced again.

"I don't know," he gritted through his teeth. "Since that mission I'm on edge, like there was something I was supposed to do and didn't. This wolf in me is driving me insane."

"You sure it's a wolf thing?" I experienced nothing like what Sean described. Humans raised me too, though at an older age than Sean. I still had memories of my original pack. The wolf thing wasn't the shock to me as to Sean. He had no clue what he was until he met up with us as a recruit in the Rangers.

"What else could it be?"

"Not sure," I admitted. "But head shrinker is above my pay grade."

"Everything is above your pay grade," he snorted.

This was close enough to one of Sean's ill-mannered jokes that I thought he might have lightened up. But then Lucius and Kyle walked in and the tension in the room jacked higher.

"Listen up," barked Lucius as he rounded the corner of the couch to take a position by the side of, but not in front of the window. Even though we shut the curtains for security reasons, our pack leader took no chances.

"We're booked on a flight to Connecticut. Sean here found Vivian's address in two seconds flat, so she's not safe right now. The cartel has computer people just as good."

"Not really," I offered. And that was damned straight because Sean was a premier computer specialist.

"Let's give them the benefit of the doubt," snarled Lucius. Damn, he was in as rotten a mood as Sean. "Robbins charged us with protecting her, and we will. So, pack up. You've got ten minutes. Our plane is waiting for us."

I cringed thinking of the expense and Kyle, on the same page as me, arched an eyebrow.

"Another private jet?" said Kyle. "This job is costing us a fortune. Are we even going to break even?"

"You let me worry about that," said Lucius vehemently. "Job one is the mission. Chop, chop."

Chop, chop was Lucius' no-nonsense signal so we got into gear. But Kyle, who worried more about money than the rest of us couldn't leave it alone.

"You know it's possible to buy a private jet for what's it's costing us in charters."

"You've got a problem, corporal? Stick it in the suggestion box."

Sean and I snigger then because Lucius' suggestion box is the place where the sun don't shine.

"When you bend over," said Kyle, "I will."

Kyle grew up with Lucius and took a few more liberties with him than Sean or I would, but even this was too far, especially with Lucius on edge. Our pack leader growled with feral intensity and Kyle held up his hands in submission.

"Okay. Okay. I get it," he said.

"Move, corporal!"

Kyle took off to his room in the suite and we went to ours and threw together our gear.

"How long will it take," said Sean with a sidelong glance to me. "To get there?"

I shrugged. "About twelve-fourteen hours with a refueling stop."

"Too long," he snarled.

"Brah, we're halfway around the world. What do you expect?"

"I expect things not to be FUBAR. We should get a private team on her before we get there."

I didn't see things as fucked up beyond all reason, but my teammate, however had a different perspective.

"Dude, we *are* the private team. Chill. If Lucius thinks she's safe enough until we get there, she is."

"I don't have to like it," he muttered.

I'd never seen Sean this worked up over any job, and it was entirely weird. What the hell; I lived with a bunch of wolf shifters. Weird was just part of the daily.

But he didn't calm down on the plane. Instead he used the Wi-Fi connection to search the web about her, and found a bunch of stuff. He was scary with his internet magic. Maybe we should call him Wizard instead of Sparks, but then that would only make him trot out his D & D board.

Dungeons and Dragons? With him as Dungeon Master? No way.

He pulled pictures from her high school yearbook, and her social media and the local paper that announced her scholarship at a small local college, and then Colorado College. She was smart, all right, and I had to admit she was pretty in a librarian sort-of way. But this gal, Vivian Blake, didn't have much info. She was normal, okay, a little more bookish than usual, but she seemed sane and healthy—though circumstances fooled me before. She's not our usual client.

Spooks pass plenty of psych evals and still end up taking crazy chances to get them killed. Or more hush-hush they take on double agent duty, or just plain run freaky ops with dubious funding. One wonders if they got approval for some of the shit they did. But you don't do ghost work unless you have some freaky corners in your brain.

Like thinking bringing an untrained asset into a dangerously volatile situation was a prime idea.

Not my place to question. I was just part of the back-up

team to yank some jerk's butt out of a life-and-death situation. It was our specialty, and what got us the big bucks.

We're on a smallish jet, so it might cost us about twenty-five grand for this ride. But it had a nice stewardess that brought us what we liked, which was a rare luxury. She handed me my whiskey, neat, with a suggestive smile and I gave her a rough one back. But I had no interest, so the matter dropped. I stared out the window thinking about jobs, lifetime earnings, money socked away for future retirement, and not blowing the future.

The seat was a nice comfortable leather, and I could put my feet up. The whiskey must be expensive because it went down smooth with a smoky aftertaste. Now if we could only stop spending money like water, I'd be perfectly happy.

How long it took to get to Vivian was total bullshit. If it would have done any good, I'd taken Sarg out and given him a beat down—if he wouldn't mash me into the ground. Lucius' sheer ability to dominate any of us made him pack Alpha. He was a strong leader, and even some of his more questionable decisions usually worked out okay.

I couldn't get Vivian out of my head, so I was more than happy to obey Lucius' directive to pull intel on her. Every picture I yanked off the internet only affirmed to me how beautiful she was. Heck, even as a teenager she was adorable, and though vaguely aware I was in deep, I didn't care. Life, as Lucius would say, was too freaking short to sweat the small stuff.

It'd been too damn long since I'd been interested in any woman, and unlike the rest the team I wasn't into anonymous hookups. Call it the way I was made. Orphaned at birth, I was adopted by a human family but I always had the sense I was different. I didn't look like the rest of the family or act like any of them, and we had too many arguments over stupid stuff. I was too wild, too argumentative, and chaffed under familial restrictions that made no sense to me.

It wasn't their fault, and it wasn't mine, but I grew up from the outside looking in, trying to conform and failed miserably. It made dating torturous - feeling the odd man out and not sure of yourself. I was more shy and awkward than anyone else and found solace in all things electronic. It did not make me date bait.

The only place I vaguely fit in was the Marines, where we were all misfits. The good thing about the Marines is that they are awesome at breaking down your resistance and molding you into the soldier they wanted. It was when I answered the call to try out for the Rangers that I found the group I'd call family. It confused then shocked me that Lucius pulled me into his team. Why would an instructor, even a temporary one, take on a newbie like me?

The night he and Kyle took Daniel and me on a special training mission was an eye-opener. When I saw Lucius and Kyle wolfing out, I freaked. I wondered if they slipped in a hallucinogen in my water. Daniel was just as confused. Kyle attacked me, and Lucius attacked Daniel—we *both* ended up shifting.

Consider me surprised.

Next thing I knew two naked men sat on the ground laughing their asses off, and both Daniel and I sat on our butts down and thumped the ground with our tails. Talk about a surreal moment.

Lucius explained who and what we were and that it was best for everyone that he took us into the pack. He'd get our assignments changed, and we'd go out as one unit. Lucius got us our first combat assignment. I don't know how the man does the things he does, but I've seen bona fide generals bow to Lucius' requests. Maybe it was a wolf thing.

Me? While learning I was a shifter relieved me of the

uncomfortable burden of trying to fit into human society, I was still trying to reconcile my head and heart with the discovery of my inner wolf. The family that raised me was so normal it was abnormal, and things like shifters did not blip their radar. Shoot, they didn't even let me watch Star Trek on the family TV because it was weird.

I couldn't stay in that life, and though they knew it, dad fought with me on the day I announced my enlistment. We hadn't spoken since. Lucius, Kyle, and Daniel were the brothers I never had, though I was closer to Daniel than the other two. Lucius and Kyle grew up in the same pack, another concept I had difficulty wrapping my head around. Seriously? Shifters living in packs in the great open spaces of the country? A whole sub-culture of people who shifted from human to animal at will? That was mind-boggling too, and I wonder how they stand the separation from their pack. And all because they banged the Alpha's daughter?

Now that was a story, and one that Daniel and I pulled from them after a long day's patrol and a bottle of whiskey Daniel scored somewhere. It wasn't pretty and a serious pile of pain that neither got over. I'd rather have a bullet rip my flesh than see one more time Kyle shift to wolf and lay there whimpering while Lucius stroked his head trying to calm him down. That's when I learned that heavy drinking and shifting do not go together and abstained from binges.

We all did.

But Vivian was a binge all her own, and I didn't understand why. My wolf thrashed within me, and that bastard was the reason I couldn't talk like a decent person to my pack mates. Looking at pictures of her made my blood run hotter than motor oil in a car, and I wanted nothing more than to get next to her. My wolf, who normally wasn't the most articulate animal kept whispering *mine, mine, mine* in a maddening loop and there was nothing I can do to shut him up. Even a jack and coke didn't settle him down. In fact, as the alcohol relaxed my body, another part of me perked up, and if the other guys see, I'd hear no end of it.

"Gather 'round," said Lucius. "We need to figure out how we are going to go about this protection detail. I want to maintain a presence in the house if we can. Otherwise, it is long patrols of the perimeter, and from what I see on the maps she lives in a densely populated area, so that is not our best option."

"What are you thinking, Alpha?" said Kyle. "A honey trap?"

I nearly growled then because I don't want any of these jokers pretending to date her.

"Not my preferred method but, Sparks, see what opportunities are there. I pulled my laptop to me and started looking for ins. Local bars and activities are good places to meet, as well as grocery stores."

"We need a base too.

"No hotels in town."

"Not optimum. Rentals?"

I flipped through the real estate listings

"Nothing short-term and expensive as hell."

"Keep looking," he said.

"I will," I said.

"So that's our plan?" said Daniel. "Set up in town and make contact."

"Any other ideas, corporal?"

"Nope," he said.

"Then that's the plan. If we have to patrol her neighborhood on foot, we will."

"Got ya," said Kyle.

The idea that we will hit her hometown soon has a curious effect on me. I couldn't wait to see her, and the thought of being next to her drove my wolf insane. Oh, fuck.

Not here, not now. My pants got tighter, and I know this wouldn't be solved by reciting baseball scores.

"Where's the head?" I asked the stewardess.

"Hey, Sparks," called Kyle. "Can I borrow your computer."

"Sure," I said. "Just leave up the porn you find for me to see."

"Dick."

Don't remind me, because that was more urgent than it should be.

The good thing about a private plane is that the amenities are better than basic and Marine squared away, as in sparkling clean. And thank god there was hand soap to smooth the way. A growl came from deep within, as I dropped my pants. I leaned against the door and pulled out my cock.

It wasn't long before I was deep in my fantasy of her and me, under a night sky filled with millions of unknowable stars. My wolf wanted to howl in satisfaction, but I tapped that down.

It was a curious disconnect to think of my wolf as different from me. He wasn't. The wolf was me, buried deep, and from him, I got my strength of body and will. As much as I wanted to pretend I'm human, the wildness of the beast drove me, and in thinking of Vivian, he was nearly ungovernable.

I could see it in my head.

She held my hand as I connected to her, the earth, and sky. My chest expanded at the power and majesty of it.

She stroked me, then palmed the head making awesome tingles spread through my body. I imagined her body under clothes and her tits bouncing as she rode me. She was so tight, so hot, and I pulled her down to me, so I could suck one of her nipples in my mouth. She gasped, and it was the sexiest thing I had ever heard.

"Fuck me," she cried, and I snapped my hips under her, pulled

her down and split her apart. And she loved it, every fucking bit of it. Her hands were on my chest and mine on her hips, and we were two people becoming one. My balls tingled and drew up, and I was almost at the point of no return.

I heard her say, "Go ahead, baby, give it all to me. Now. I want it, all of you."

Mine, my wolf said again and a vision flashed through my head of me, Vivian, and children. This is what he wanted, what I wanted—a mate to call my own, and the wolf inside tells me Vivian is it, my mate.

All I had to do was claim her.

KYLE

"What are we waiting for, Kyle?" Lucius growled at me. "Where's our shuttle?" We stood outside on the lower deck for arrivals at Bradley, and I glanced at my watch.

"I couldn't get a shuttle," I deadpanned. It took all I had not to grin because what was coming was awesome. That didn't mean I wouldn't rattle Lucius' cage; he's been wound tighter than a spring since Colombia.

Maybe we took too many missions in a row. Lucius liked to load on the work this time of year. August always got to him because of what happened to us fourteen years ago. I'm over it mostly, though get a good drink on and I'm not fit for human or beastly company. We bonded with Aleesha, despite what her father said and there were times that still I missed her.

For Lucius, it was worse. He'd loved her since she came into the world. The adults thought it was adorable that he'd guard her while she slept. The adults didn't take Lucius' overprotectiveness seriously so when her father, our Alpha, announced the mating agreement with a rival pack, Lucius went nuts. We took off with Aleesha, who didn't like the forced mating idea any more than we did. The Alpha found us and claimed his daughter back, and that was the end of her rebellion and our time with our pack. No one understood what we did. Even my father, the pack shaman, didn't stick up for me, which sucked.

Seriously, I didn't think Lucius would make it out of those dark days. We wandered, ate off the land, and avoided humans. The winter was especially tough, the smaller game scarce and the bigger game much too hard for two scrawny teenage wolves to bring down. We wandered into a human military recruiting office at the lure of hotdogs, donuts, and coffee.

That, and one unscrupulous recruiter later, is how we ended up in the army.

We had each other, which was our only blessing. Whenever someone got a wild hair to separate us, Lucius would pull what I call his 'Alpha trick,' and get things turned around. The things the man did was incredible. Not that I'd tell him directly. His head was big enough as it was.

"What bullshit did you pull now, Kyle?" Lucius growled.

"Me?" I said with innocence in my voice. Lucius had to blow off some steam. My little surprise should be the perfect thing.

"Dude," said a confused Sean as he joined us on the outer cement island of the arrivals underpass. Across from us, the four-story parking garage rose, separated by two lanes of one-way traffic. "Where's our luggage? I waited forever for it to come off the turnstiles."

"I sent it ahead to our hotel," I said.

Daniel cuffed Sean in the chest, though Daniel was confused too. Only he figured out right away to get intel he had to find me. "Get with the program."

"Would be easier," complained Sean, "if someone bothered to inform me what the program was."

"We're checked in already?" rumbled Lucius suspiciously.

"Yes, Sir!" I said militarily. "I thought you might want to do recon before we settled in."

Before he could question me further, the straight truck I waited for pulled up into the arrival lane. The guy hopped out of the cab.

"You the Fire Team?" he said.

"Yep."

"Let's get this done, quick. I've never done a drop-off at the airport, and I'm not sure security will like this."

I nodded. They appeared to be strict here and quickly waived cars forward that waited in the arrival lane without someone loading luggage.

"What is this, Kyle?" said Lucius.

Sean peered in as the driver rolled up the tailgate.

"Wicked!"

"What?" said Daniel. "Wow, this is above and beyond, Kyle."

The truck driver rolled off four different models of Harley's, one by one off the hydraulic lift.

"And you complained about money," said Lucius as I looked at the paperwork and took the keys.

"They aren't expensive," I replied as I checked over the contracts. "Hey, dude, forgetting something?"

"Oh, yeah." The guy went to the cab and pulled out a garment bag.

"Merry fucking Christmas," I said as I opened the bag and tossed a leather jacket at each of them. A security guard gave us the stink-eye as we pulled on the jackets.

"And the helmets, remember."

"Yeah. You know they're not required in Connecticut."

"We're into safety."

"Fine."

Once the helmets were handed out, the truck driver, seeing the stink-eye the security guard gave us, hightailed into the truck and took off.

"Let's roll," I said as I tossed key fobs at each of them. "Sean, you get the Street model, that's the all-black beauty there. It's the newest of the lineup. Daniel, you get the Soft Tail."

"Why do I get the Soft Tail?"

"Guess," I said tossing him the keys. The guys sniggered, even Lucius. You would think we were eighteen instead of our late twenties.

"Sarg, you get the Dyna Wide Glide."

"Why does he get the Wide Glide?" smart-assed Daniel said.

"Guess," I said.

"Hah!" said Sean hopping on the bike and. "Last one there buys dinner. First one picks it."

"Shit," said Daniel, scrambling to mount his bike; everyone knew how much Sean liked expensive restaurants. Sean had an early lead, but that wouldn't last long. We'd catch up to them fast enough.

Lucius put his fist into my chest.

"Way to go to keep a low profile," he grumbled.

"You've got a better way to explain four men that eat, sleep and live together blowing into a new town?"

"Is that what made you think of this?"

I shook my head. "Nope."

"Then what?"

"Fun."

He raised an eyebrow.

"You remember what *fun* is like, don't you? Doing something you enjoy? Letting loose?"

"No."

"It's time you remember," I said as I climbed onto the motorcycle. "So glad you're buying dinner."

Gauntlet thrown. It didn't take him long to catch up to me, and we flew down the interstate faster than we should. There was nothing like the wind in your face and the sensation of the world rushing past with nothing between it and you, besides the rubber of your tires on the road. It was touch and go around Hartford because the traffic was heavy as fuck, but once we got off 91-South and onto 9-South, the ride eased up considerably. Aside from two ill-placed traffic lights, it was a straight shot down to Frankton along a lightly traveled road nestled between the Connecticut hills.

Daniel howled while Sean flipped me off as I passed them but they both smiled too. This ride was as cleansing as a baptismal dip in the River Jordan. While not a run in the moonlight, it unleashed the wildness held prisoner inside during the hectic schedule Lucius built the past few months.

We vied for the lead position on the road, while Lucius hung back allowing this competition for the sake of our wolfish souls. That was until Lucius overtook us and turned down the exit for Frankton.

Damn it. He was hot dogging it again.

He wasn't immediately visible as we navigated the sharp turn off the exit. Consider it pack instinct, but we always needed to keep our Alpha in sight. Him taking off was his way to yank our chains and remind us who the Alpha was.

Brown rock rose on either side of us as we roared down the road, the sounds of our engines bouncing off the walls amplifying the rumbles to the roar of thunder.

Sean took the left-hand turn onto the main road indicated by the traffic signs, and we followed. Picturesque Victorian houses flashed on either side of the road between tall oaks and tall weeds of different varieties. It was a pretty place, but we didn't have time to look. Lucius was ahead, and the instinct of the pack was to find him.

An aroma hit my nose, and I knew where he was. It came from the right-hand side of the road, and I hand-signed our right-hand turn. We slowed and rumbled into the gravel parking lot of a restaurant simply called *Breakfast Nook*. That sounded like more than a fine idea. I slowed to let Sean and Daniel pull ahead in a burst of last-minute one-ups-man-ship.

"BS!" called Sean as he pulled off his helmet. "Why'd you fall back, Kyle?"

"I'm not as good a rider as you and F. K."

"Screw that."

I shrugged. "What did you care? Unless you want to pay?"

"No," said Sean. "But I would have chosen a nicer place. Besides, we should get to Vivian's digs."

"We need to recon and discuss our options, and I, for one, don't want to do that without coffee," I replied.

The restaurant was quiet, and I wondered if the food was any good. But when it comes to eats, I didn't judge. I'd eaten better and worse across the globe.

Lucius already had his coffee before him, as well as a local newspaper. We sat with him with, shuffling a few chairs over, and the waitress brought us coffee and took our orders.

"I'd hit that," Daniel said with a nod of his head to the waitress.

"You'd hit anything," scoffed Lucius. He continued to stare at the paper with a thoughtful expression on his face.

"I think I found our in."

"Which is?" I said.

He turned the paper around.

"There's an ad here for renting rooms at the address we have for Vivian."

"What?" said Sean. He looked affronted, probably because he didn't find this out online.

"Settle Sparks. The paper was only printed today. Says to come by. No phone number."

"Wow," I said. "It couldn't be more perfect."

"We'll see," said Lucius. "After breakfast."

VIVIAN

*C*uriously, when the plane landed in the US, my passport waited for me at the airport, trotted out by a terminal employee. Thus, we were spared the hassle of trying to explain why I entered the country without it. A different problem presented itself: I didn't have a ride home, so the airplane guy—Pete—ordered a shuttle and put me in it.

"Give me your business card, and I'll pay you back."

"Don't worry about it. I'll charge it to the Fire Team."

I found myself at home, alone. The silence was deafening. Not hearing Nona's warm voice, or her bustling about the house doing one task after another crushed me. And then when I found the stack of bills stuffed in Nona's utility drawer in the kitchen, I knew I had bigger problems than what to do with the house that was in sad disrepair. To add salt to the wound, I got the hospital bill for her final days yesterday. I stared at all the bills spread out on the kitchen table with the same sense of futility I had when I first saw them. There were pieces of paper for Nona's cremation, and the utilities, and a property tax and water bill. The whole fucking world looked like one big dollar sign bashing me over the head.

Because Nona had let the bills slip big time in her last couple months, and the phone was disconnected, I had to use the neighbor's phone to beg the electric company not to shut off service. At least they were more reasonable than the phone company, who didn't honor reconnect requests on landlines anymore. They were deliberately phasing them out because most everyone had cell phones or VOIP service through their cable. Nona didn't believe in cable, or television in general, and my computer and cell phone were left behind in Colombia anyway. Like that mysterious big man in Colombia said, I had to choose my life or my shit—*shit* was replaceable, but my life was not.

It was too much, and you couldn't blame a gal for crying. I lost my grandmother, my only family in the world, and had zero income to take care of any of these responsibilities. Already I'd had two people look at the house in response to my ad to rent rooms only to have them turn it down. Seeing the condition of the place, and the lack of a working bathroom on the second floor was a real deal breaker.

A knock on the door brought my head up from where I cradled it in my arms on the table. Oh god, I couldn't look like this for potential renters. Quickly splashing my face with water, I hurried to the door.

I needn't have bothered rushing. There stood Nash Turner, Nona's lawyer. Oh, dear lord, what did he want now? He gobbled enough of my day yesterday going over every single issue with the house concluding it was barely fit for occupation.

"Hey, Vivian," he said in much too friendly a tone. "Can I come in?"

No! The last thing I wanted was grandma's smarmy

lawyer in the house. I didn't like him or the vibe he gave off and did not want to deal with him.

"Sure. What's that?" I said pointing to the black box under his arm.

"Oh, right. Yeah. These are her ashes. The funeral home sent them to me."

"Thanks," I said as I took them. I stood there in the foyer, hoping my immobility discouraged him from walking past me.

"So, have you looked over those probate papers? I'd like to get them filed."

"No, sorry. I've been a bit busy."

"Right. Well, if you want clear title to sell the house, I need to submit them to the probate court."

Why was he so anxious to rush the probate and sell the house? It didn't feel right.

"I'm not sure I am selling the house."

"But we talked about this yesterday. The repairs were too much for your grandmother to handle."

"That may be, but I don't see the reason to rush. Because of all this, I've deferred my next semester."

When I talked the Dean Wimbly of Academic Affairs, he strongly suggested that after Colombia they would have to review my qualifications again, as if I was to blame for Professor Robbins' disappearance. Everything was up in the air, from whether I would start school again in two weeks, or even if I still had my scholarships. It was just one more black cherry on the Sundae of my life.

"Besides, aren't we moving the probate too fast? I'm still getting hospital bills."

"Vivian," sighed Nash. "I hate to say this, but I've been doing work for your grandmother for a while. And I need to get paid too."

Of course. Everyone wanted their money.

Before we could discuss this further, a shadow fell over the frosted glass of the oval insert in the heavy oak door, and a knock shattered the tense atmosphere between Nash and me. I opened the door to see a four hulking men, all of them over six feet on the porch. I peered around them to see four shiny, and I mean off the showroom floor *sparkling* bright Harleys. Despite the road-weary expression on the men's faces, their bikes and clothes shouted money.

It was the tallest of them that stood forward. His dark hair was buzzed cut, and his piercing green eyes sliced through me. The man easily cleared six feet easy, dwarfing my 5'6" frame. On his right stood a blond with blue eyes who was only an inch shorter than him, and his left, a sandy-haired man with hazel eyes. Behind him stood the shortest yet, if you call monster tall *short.* He smiled at me though with a broad, friendly smile as if I should recognize him.

"Can I help you with something?"

"You have four rooms to rent, which is lucky because we need four rooms."

"Listen here," piped up Nash. "You can just move on. Vivian doesn't need the likes of you in her house."

The big man tilted his head down as if he were looking over the rims of a pair of eyeglasses.

"And you are?"

"Nash Turner, Vivian's lawyer."

"Her lawyer," he said with a deadly calm that made me shiver. "*Just* her lawyer."

"Yes," I said quickly. "And he was just leaving."

"Vivian, you should consider—"

"We'll talk about it later," I said guiding Nash toward the door by his elbow.

"I really shouldn't leave you alone with a gang of bikers."

"Four hardly constitutes a gang," I said. *Yes, it is,* but I wasn't listening. Just using them to propel Nash out of the house made them worth more than gold to me. Didn't hurt they were easy on the eyes. After all I'd been through, didn't I deserve a little eye candy?

Idiot, idiot, idiot. My brain desperately signaled that danger was ahead, but I didn't care. I looked up into the front man's eyes as Nash walked glancing over his shoulder down the stairs.

"Would you care to come inside and see the house?"

"Yes, we would like that very much," he rumbled. Why did his voice sound familiar?

"Excuse me, do I know you?"

"I think I would remember a beautiful woman like you," he said easily.

He strode into the house, confidence and strength oozing through every pore, and I felt the need to fan my face. If he wasn't hot enough to melt my insides having three more follow him did. I didn't think I could look at the other three directly because I just might spontaneously combust.

I led him into the living room to the left and crossed to the fireplace and put Nona's ashes on the mantel.

Concern crossed his face as if he'd seen funeral urns before.

"Someone close?" he asked.

"My grandmother. She died while—" The breath in my chest suddenly fled and I swallowed hard. "Anyway, she didn't tell me how sick she was, otherwise I wouldn't have gone… out of the country."

It crossed my mind that I was still on the run in the sense that the people who chased me in the first place were associated with a big drug cartel. It didn't seem wise to give lots of details to my life. A scant whisper of doubt crossed my mind that these people could be dangerous.

"Excuse me," said the blond with a huge smile. "Big guy here hasn't made introductions. This guy is Lucius Chambers, that guy is Daniel Oberon, and short stuff there is Sean Chase. And I'm Kyle Dean."

"Nice to meet you."

"And we are very pleased to meet you, Vivian."

"So," I said making a stab at being a responsible renter. "What do you do for work?"

"Private security, mostly, though for the next month we are off."

"You are? I mean, that must be awesome you can afford to miss a month of work."

"We need the break," said Kyle. "We spent the past nine months on the road."

"Who do you do security for? Anyone I'd know?"

Lucius frowned.

"I mean, anyone famous?"

"The people we protect usually don't want to be famous," said Lucius.

"Here's the thing," said Kyle. "It's not easy to find rentals for four guys in August here. It seems to be rental frenzy month for students, and we haven't found a single place that suits us."

"And," said Lucius, "you mentioned something in the ad about rent in exchange for work?"

"I did? Yes, I did. How are you guys on plumbing? The second-floor shower is out, and the first-floor half bath's toilet doesn't work."

"Plumbing's my thing," said Daniel.

"In the service, you pick up skills," said Lucius.

"Oh, you served in the military?"

"At one time," said Lucius simply. He put his hand on the poorly peeling wallpaper next to the fireplace.

"I can offer half on the rent, for help."

Lucius nodded gravely.

"Can we move in right away?"

"Sure."

"Okay, Vivian, you have a deal."

LUCIUS

I woke up with a start as the sun streamed through the windows that Sean cleaned last night. Leave it to Sean to throw himself into cleaning. I don't know how they torture those jarheads on Parris Island, but most of them are forever warped with a cleaning fetish. Even for him, Sean threw himself into this cover project with more enthusiasm than I expected.

It was quiet, too much so; I wasn't used to sleeping in a place that's this white bread normal. I was used to the hubbub of foreign cities, exotic smells from local foods, and the syncopated rhythms of cultural music. The rattle of lawnmowers, birds chattering outside my window, or the aroma of coffee wafting up the stairs from below was unfamiliar to me.

Though... *Coffee.*

Now *that* was a singular motivation to pull my ass out of bed.

"Hey, Alpha," said Kyle sunnily as I stumbled into the kitchen. "The coffee's on the counter, and the food's on the way."

"Oh?" I said pouring a cup.

"Yeah, Vivian went into town for groceries."

"What?" I growled. "You let her leave to go into public places?"

"Calm down, Jean Luc. Daniel is with her."

I glared. Jean Luc was what he called me when he wanted to get me riled. He knew I hated all things Star Trek, and apparently I was the only person on earth that did. Or so he tells me.

"*Still.*"

"Still, nothing. Drink your coffee, and I'll give you a sit rep."

"I did an eval of the property. Weird shit here. Some of the plumbing is damaged, as if someone deliberately fucked up repairs. Daniel will get that fixed today. I've rented a truck so we can haul supplies."

"For a man complaining about the money you're leaning hard on the company card."

Kyle grimaced.

"The budget got blown when you rented that private charter. I don't know why you did that. The commercial jet left only two hours later."

"You checked that."

"I did."

"Seemed important to get here."

"Yeah, Sean said the same thing."

"So, here's the list of repairs that need to be made."

Kyle slid the pad to me, and I glanced at it.

"What's the cost for supplies."

"Viv's paying for that."

"Out of the money we gave her."

"Are you getting ill over this? Because it was your plan. Plus, we have to sleep somewhere, it's cheaper here than a hotel, and we've slept in worse."

I rubbed my jaw. It was my plan, but something irked me about this whole situation, and I couldn't put my finger on it. My nostrils flared as I became aware of a faint but distinct odor. It unsettled me, and my wolf paced within as if I should pay attention to it.

"What's that smell?" I said.

"What smell?" said Kyle staring at that damned pad of his.

I don't know. It seems to be everywhere. Maybe it was indigenous to this house, the conflation of wood, linoleum, paints, and food seeped into a structure over a hundred years old.

"Never mind. So, I take it no sign of the cartel or threats against Vivian?"

"Not so far. I've checked with security at the airport and no one suspicious hit their radar." He shrugged his shoulder. "There is a good amount of gang activity in this state though, so the LI might send some of the local soldiers."

"Don't call them soldiers," I growled. "They don't deserve that dignity. They're thugs."

"Message received Alpha. So, I'm thinking that in this town where only 2.7% are Hispanic anyone blowing into town matching that profile will stick out like a sore thumb. We should have one of us run errands on a regular basis and keep an eye out on Main Street."

"Check," I reply.

The back door opened and Daniel walked in hauling bags of groceries. Vivian followed and that scent wafted in with her. Oh hell, it was her that gave it off. Instantly my wolf strained to get closer to it, and I growled again.

"Okay, Boss?" said Daniel.

"Don't call me Boss," I snarled.

"Get him another cup of coffee, F.K. One cup isn't going to do today."

"Oh?" said Vivian as she pulled her grocery items from the bag. "Did you sleep okay, Lucius?"

The solicitous tone in her voice, like she cared, did funny things to my insides. It had been a damn long time since any woman cared, not since Aleesha.

Suddenly, I wanted Vivian to care.

Nope. Not happening. I didn't care how attractive she was, though her curves had me downshifting to navigate them. I was all-too aware of how my pack was crowding her. Sean touched her back as he moved to put away some groceries. Daniel pushed him away from her, and Kyle watched all this with overt interest. I could practically see Kyle's inner wolf pinning back his ears.

And Vivian? Her face flushed with all the attention. Her eyes shone with that special look of a woman interested in a man—only they shone that way when she looked at each of us.

Oh, *hell* no.

This could get messy fast with these guys competing for one woman. I wouldn't let Vivian, as attractive as she was, destroy the cohesion of my unit. We'd worked too hard to build what we have.

"F.K., Sparks, I'm sure you have something else to do than get into Miss Vivian's way."

Daniel frowned. "I'm just helping her so we can get breakfast on the table. Here, Sparks, peel these potatoes." He shoved a bag of potatoes into Sparks' hands.

"The whole bag?"

"Yes."

"Damn," he muttered. But he sat at the table and pulled out a switchblade to do the job.

"I'll handle the toast," said Kyle.

And like the well-trained unit they were, breakfast was on the table in forty-five minutes. It was complete with toast, potatoes, bacon and eggs—all while I glared at the lot of them, thinking about assassins and team members distracted by a female. I saw we needed to finish this mission up quick and get on to our next job.

That fate of my pack depended on it.

DANIEL

$\mathcal{W}$e had a choice of north or south to catch big box supply store, and I chose south as the marginally closer location. Kyle, our logistics man, assessed the roof as needing some minor repairs; it was nothing we couldn't handle. One stair on the front steps had to be replaced; again a small fix to a problem that would only get worse over time. Mostly, the house needed paint, inside and out, a few holes in the wall patched, shingles replaced and some fair to middling plumbing. Not too bad but jobbed out to a contractor would cost at least ten grand. I could see where an elderly person couldn't come up with that kind of cash.

Kyle wrote up a list of supplies and put in an order online for me to pick up. I probably should have brought one of the guys, but I wanted some time to think for myself.

I didn't mind helping Vivian out. That was one fine looking woman, and if I could only get Sean from beating my time with her, I might have a chance. The problem was, he was always there. If it wasn't him, it was Kyle grinning at her like the big bad wolf and Lucius who just glared at all of us to keep us in line.

Well, screw him. We didn't get much downtime as it was, and lately none at all. I deserve R & R. Or at least a little time with an interesting woman. Who cared if she was the client —well, not technically, because Robbins was our client, but she was the principal on this leg, so it should be hands off.

So why *isn't* it? Why did my wolf sniff after her like she was in heat? I mean, she was human, so she couldn't be in heat. Kyle told me that shifter women do that, though only a couple times a year if they didn't get pregnant. He also said shifter women didn't use birth control so if you mated with one you would have pups and that concept alone blew my mind. Growing up human instead of shifter left me unprepared for these aspects of shifter society. Perhaps it was better that we lived mostly as humans.

Well, except when the moon rose. When that happened, the call of prey was just too much. Shifting was an awesome release, one where I got to run with my pack and experience the sheer joy of being one with the earth and sky.

What did that mean for Vivian and me if I did get close to her? I didn't have to worry about random hook-up in the past, but this didn't feel like a random hook-up. This was a game changer, and it had deep consequences for me and my pack. Did this mean that if Vivian and I did hook up, I'd have to leave the pack? I could see where Sean would be pissed at me majorly and Kyle and Lucius would be none too pleased.

Thinking about the story of how Lucius and Kyle got kicked from their birth pack, and how they still stung from it, I didn't know if I could live through it even with a wonderful woman on my arm. Didn't help that my career and financial fortunes were tied with the pack. While I'd put away some dough, it wasn't enough to set me for life. How would I earn a living? All these things played through my mind as I pulled up to the store and loaded the supplies. I decided to do a little personal recon at the local bar.

Alcohol and shifter metabolism didn't go well, so it was best to go easy. I sat and scanned the bar, looking at the patrons as I sipped my beer. A pretty blue-eyed gal sat next to me.

"Hey," she said. "I haven't seen you here before."

"That's right. I'm just here temporarily."

"Really? I like temporary."

I glanced at her again, but something curious happened—or rather, didn't. Though she was just my type, I had zero interest. Nada. *Zip.*

This was very strange. In fact, I'd rather get in a fist fight with a grizzly bear than get up close and personal.

"Sorry, I have to get home."

Wow. Whoa. *Home?* When have I referred to a place as home?

My brain was taking some weird turns.

"Okay, big guy. If you change your mind…"

She let her words trail off suggestively, and there was a place the human part of my brain that is kicking me in the cojones. This potential hookup looked fast, easy and without ties, the guy trifecta, and my wolf would have *none* of it.

That bastard.

Home.

I wasn't a big believer in my wolf talking to me, as Kyle and Lucius claimed theirs did. Here he was using *words* to convey a thought and emoting like crazy, like he was a puppy looking for treats.

Oh, fucking hell, this was worse than I thought.

I climbed back in the huge Ford double cab we rented and headed back to Vivian's house.

The unmistakable aroma of grilling meat met my nose as my boots hit the driveway. If I'd shifted, I was certain my tail would wag. I followed my nose to the back of the house and see the guys and Vivian sitting on the porch with plates on their laps.

"Daniel," said Vivian brightly. "We saved you a plate."

"Yeah," groused Sean. "Next time don't be late."

"Excuse me. I didn't get the memo about lunch."

"What memo?" said Kyle.

"Always looking out for me, that's my—" I stopped then when Lucius gave me a cautionary stare. "That's my good buddies. Where's that plate."

After lunch, Kyle helped her clean up while Lucius, Sean and I started on repairs. Kyle took the roof, and Sean helped me with the plumbing which was a nasty job, because the basement had a dirt floor, and the pipes were corroded and brittle.

When I saw him hauling his laundry down to the washer and dryer sitting there, I got the clue why he volunteered to help me.

"What?" I said. "You can't stand a day's stink on your clothes?"

"And you can?" he snorted. "Besides I thought it would be a good idea to test out the water system."

"Your sense of cleanliness is weird." I snorted.

"And your nose is shot," he said as he fingered one of the long, short basement windows that lined the outside wall. "How can you stand the moldy stench in here."

He pried the window from years of crust and tried to prop it open but found the elbow hinge that did had broken. Sean snatched a stay piece of wood from the floor and angled it to do the job.

"Dude, all you are going to do is let bugs in."

"So, I'm trading one evil for another," he said. "I'm picking my battles here."

The pipes going to the washer and dryer were good. It

looked like they were recently installed. There were a couple of leaks at some joints, but I fixed them with solder. The rest of the pipes in the basement? Not so good.

"Damn. I'm going to have to replumb the whole thing," I said as another piece of pipe cracked under my wrench.

"Yeah. You should return that copper pipe we bought and get PVC piping. That will last longer than metal down here." Sean slammed the door to the dryer several times to try to get it to shut, so I had to fix that so Sean's clothes wouldn't morph into a moldy mess in the August heat and this damp New England basement.

Unfortunately, the plumbing was shot to hell for the day because it was getting late, and Lucius wanted all of us to guard the house as evening settled in.

Lucius sent Sean and Kyle off on various patrols of the property. Kyle left to do a recon of the wider area, and I was on rest shift. Because I had the midnight to dawn patrol, I lounged in my room trying to catch some rack time when I smelled smoke.

After hastily pulling on sweats I flew down the stairs. Smoke poured out of the fireplace in a gush of black smoke, and Vivian stood at the window trying to open it.

"I can't open this window," she complained.

We had sealed all the windows in the house since an open window was a security concern, but obviously, I couldn't tell her that since she didn't know why we were here.

Finding the flue handle, I pushed it up and the smoke stopped pouring into the living room. Fortunately, the central air—the only thing that seemed to work right in this house—dissipated the foul air quickly.

"Daniel," said Vivian breathlessly. "Thank you."

The flush on her face and that breathless voice were damn sexy. Too sexy. I should turn around and go back upstairs.

"What were you trying to do?"

"Nona and I would toast marshmallows in the fireplace." She held out a bag of marshmallows and a long skewer. "I was missing her, and even though it's August, I thought if I—"

"The flue is open now. You won't have a problem with the smoke."

"Thanks," she said blowing a tendril of hair from her face. That one action fascinated me, or rather my wolf, and I couldn't stop staring at her. That said, continuing to do was rude, so I had to move into a diversionary tactic.

"Do you have another one of those skewers?"

Soon we sat in front of the fireplace carefully turning our marshmallows, though they weren't the only things getting hot. Sitting next to Vivian had me wanting to get closer.

"So, what's your theory on marshmallow roasting?" she said. "Slow and even browning or a flaming char."

"Flaming char, for sure." I stuck it into the fire and watched it flare and bubble before it turned black. When that happened, I yanked it out and blew out the flame. I haven't done anything like this for years not since I was a boy and I went camping with a school friend. The acrid coating hit my tongue first and lingered as I scarfed the melty sweet insides. It was its version of sweet and sour. I'd forgotten this taste.

Vivian wrinkled her nose. "Yuck. Now, this is the way to roast a marshmallow. Nice and brown, crispy on the outside, melty on the inside."

"Let me see," I said. Then I leaned in and sucked it into my mouth.

"Hey!" she said in mock protest. "You stole my marshmallow."

"I'll make you a new one."

She gave me a skeptical glance as I stuck another one on

her skewer and held it over the small flame licking through the sticks she used to build the fire.

"You think I lack patience," I said.

"Usually the char broilers do."

"But you see, in my work, it's all about patience. Lots of waiting." I twisted the skewer slowly enough to let the sides brown but not enough to allow one side overheat so the marshmallow would fall off.

"Oh?"

"Sure. Keeping alert while nothing is happening is a kind of an art form. You have to stay focused on your surroundings, and not let your mind wander."

"And are you?"

"Am I?"

"Focused on your surroundings."

I yanked the browned marshmallow from the fire and glanced at her. Our eyes met and locked. I was mesmerized by that liquid brown, warm and inviting. I was so very aware that her breath hitched, and that her tongue slid across her dusty rose lips leaving them shining.

"I would say so. Here," I said holding the toasted marshmallow toward her.

"You're not going to give me the skewer?"

In all this, our bodies inched toward each other magnetically. Then, our thighs bumped into each other, and an electric shock went through me. Her words hit me at the same time, and my thoughts did not turn to marshmallows.

Show me what you can do with those lips, baby.

"No."

I held out the marshmallow invitingly, and she peered at me through her thick eyelashes, and my heart flipped flopped. After pursing her lips, she touched them delicately to the marshmallow as it started to melt off the skewer.

"Take it," I said. "Or it will fall."

Her tongue peeked out and licked the underside of the toasted confection; I couldn't take this anymore. I need that tongue in my mouth or mine in hers.

With a flick of that sexy tongue, the marshmallow entered her mouth, and my wolf rumbled his approval that she took food from us.

Mine.

Alright. Opportunity was nigh and there was no way I wasn't going for it.

"Some of it dripped on your chin," I said. I swiped the dribble with my finger and offered it to her.

Vivian's face flushed as her tongue licked my finger.

I curled my middle finger and my thumb under her delicate chin and lifted it, so our eyes met again. I lost my words then because those eyes were the most gorgeous I'd ever seen. Leaning forward I slanted my mouth to hers and met those plush lips.

She was delicious, perfect. Vivian slid her arms around my neck to draw me closer. I was hungry for her and her for me; before we knew it, our tongues writhed against each other. God, I wanted her and I wasn't thinking about where we were, or where my pack mates were. There was just me and her and a connection that was so hot, my spine sizzled and my toes curled from a simple kiss.

I froze as a warning growl came out of nowhere.

I was supposed to watch the perimeter but my inner wolf was antsy and wanted to come out; I spent far too much time keeping him contained. Usually, this happened when danger is present, but I didn't see, hear or sniff anything that signaled an intruder. I'd been out here for two hours, and things had been fine until now.

I flicked my gaze to Daniel's window on the second floor. He was supposed to be sleeping, and the window was dark but something in me couldn't trust him. I saw how he looked at my mate.

This whole *mate* thing was new to me, and my human side had trouble wrapping my head around the idea. My wolf, however. He insisted, and his instincts were always good, so I had to roll with this and see where it took me.

No way would I let Daniel get next to Vivian. I didn't like that he was in the house with her. Pacing by the boxwood hedges at the edge of the property I kept glancing at the house. I had more discipline than to go marching in to see what's going on, didn't I?

I sniffed at the smoke coming up the chimney and

wondered why someone started a fire in the middle of August. I'd served in the Sandbox so Connecticut's August heat didn't bother me, but it was odd someone deliberately lit a fire now.

Yes. Damn odd. *Suspicious.* Maybe even *dangerous.*

That's what my wolf held to, and before I knew it, I had burst into the house. Smoke hung in the air, and I rushed toward a concentration of the aroma. I scent burnt sugar, and my wolf's hackles rose, recognizing before me that another male had offered food to my mate. When I see Daniel on top of my mate, holding her down with his mouth on hers, a deep growl rumbled from my chest. Daniel turned his eyes toward me—they narrowed, like I'm his enemy.

I may well be.

"Get away from her."

"I don't think so, brah. You need to chill."

"She's mine."

"Look again. I'm here, and it is you standing in the doorway."

"Come, Vivian," I said offering my hand.

She stared at me, her cheeks flushed, and my wolf couldn't understand why our mate didn't join us. Vivian shook her head, clearly confused. I swear if that jerk marked her and confused her as to who her mate was, I'd pound him into the ground.

Daniel put his arm around her waist.

"Don't worry. Sean gets a little worked up sometimes."

I couldn't take him touching her or speaking to her like he had the right to. I growled again.

"Really, brah. Get a grip," said Daniel.

Get a grip? Oh hell no. My spring toward Daniel in my human form turned into a leap as I transformed into a wolf.

Vivian shrieked as I landed on Daniel, and she scooted against the wall. The only thought on my mind is Daniel, shifted into his own wolfish form as I took him down. Daniel snarled, and we twisted on floor snapping at each other, trying to sink fangs into fur.

I could hear my mate screaming and I felt the fear as it rolled off her, but I had no time to parse her words. I had put this interloper down first. I snarled, deep and long as Daniel thrashed. He twisted under me and broke my hold on him, but it sent him into a table by the window next to the fireplace. With a loud, shattering crash, a lamp fell and scattered glass from its base on the floor and flying into the air.

Daniel shook his fur to dislodge glass and then stood and bared his teeth at me, and I snarled back.

"Get out! Get out!" screamed Vivian. She swung the fireplace poker and brandished it like a weapon. I whirled to avoid it, and Daniel leaped on my back and clamped his mouth on my shoulder.

I yelped when his fangs pierced my fur and drew blood.

"What the hell is this!"

Vivian dropped the poker which fell with a dull thump on the wood floor and back into the wall.

Lucius and Kyle stood in the door with their guns drawn and stared at us, and instantly both of us put our heads on our paws. Lucius anger radiated hotter than the sun.

"Wha—what? Who? How?" said Vivian. She was in total shock.

"That is what I would like to know. Sean, Daniel, shift!"

"Oh my god, oh my god," Vivian shrieked as we changed.

"Look at you!" said Lucius staring at our ripped tee shirts. Our jeans had fallen off in the melee, and we scrambled to put them on.

"Wha—what just happened." Vivian's face was as white as snow.

"Kyle, get her a glass of water."

"I'll get it," I said.

"Attention, corporal! Do not move. Both of you."

On, reflex, both of us snapped to attention, and Vivian blinked as if seeing us for the first time.

"I'll be right back, Sarg," said Kyle.

Lucius moved to Vivian and took her hand. "Come sit on the couch. We have a few things to tell you."

Gently he led her to the couch and she sat gingerly as if she were glass that would break at the least pressure. Maybe she was. Humans often have a very difficult time learning about shifters.

"You did not hallucinate any of that," he said. "These two idiots showed you what we are, and that should not have happened."

"We?" she said her voice rising. "You're one of them too?"

Kyle returned with a glass of water. "Here you go, Vivian," he said. She took it and drank watching us warily over the lip of her glass.

"Yes," said Lucius gravely. "And I'm sorry. We keep a low profile because shifter numbers are so much smaller than human."

"Shifter numbers? How many are there?'

"We don't know for sure because we don't count our numbers. Maybe a half million in the world? We live a long time, and don't have many females."

Vivian gulped the rest of her water staring ahead.

"Most of us," Lucius continued, "live in packs in the great stretches of uninhabited lands. Some are native tribes, others not. But we tend to avoid human populations."

"Umm, huh," she uttered. "And you don't because?"

"Our pack disowned Kyle and me. Daniel landed in a human foster pack after his own got destroyed. For whatever reason, Sean's parents left him as an orphan at a human orphanage. We all ended up in the service and that's where we joined up."

"So, you're in the service?"

"No more. We're private contractors now."

"Which," said Kyle, "is where we met you, so to speak."

Vivian looked as if she's ready to explode.

"What the hell do you mean by that!"

"Excuse me, corporal. I'll handle this."

"Yes, Sarg."

"It means," continued Lucius, "that your professor told us to extract you first at great danger to himself."

"So, you know where Rick is?"

"Officially, no one knows where the professor is. It's safer that way. He took something from the local cartel, and they want it back."

"Why would he do such a thing?"

Lucius and Kyle passed glances while I kept my mouth shut. I was in enough trouble with my Alpha. Daniel decided to smarten up too, the jerk.

"We can't say, Ma'am."

"Ma'am, Ma'am." Vivian seized upon the word and shook it around like a dog worrying a toy. "You come into my home under pretenses and you have the nerve to call me Ma'am. Like that will make everything okay. Well, it's not. Not at all. I want you, all of you, out of here."

No, that was not a good idea at all. We couldn't let her do that.

"Vivian—"

"Shut it, corporal," ordered Lucius. "I'll be dealing with you both soon."

Vivian's eyes narrowed.

"If Sean has something to say—"

"Sean has nothing to say. He broke some long-standing rules, and he'll pay for it, or rather both of them will. I can only apologize for their behavior."

"And what about your behavior?"

"Mine?"

"Ordering them around like they are your soldiers. Who died and made you God?"

"Um, we did," said Kyle.

"Say what?"

"We're a wolf pack, and he's our Alpha. In a way, we've chosen him as our leader."

"That's right," said Daniel. "We may not like it sometimes, but to us, it makes sense that he keeps order. Otherwise, our animal natures might run too loose."

"Did I ask for your help?" growled Lucius.

Daniel straightened his spine. "Sir, no Sir."

"Sir, Ma'am, this is all too weird for me. I want you all to leave."

"That's not a good idea," said Kyle.

"Your professor sent us here to protect you. Whatever it is he took, he put on your person, and from everything we know the cartel is sending people to take it back."

KYLE

aniel and Sean mucked things up good. Vivian, the poor woman, was in shock and ready to have a nervous breakdown. Hey, I'd seen a human girl or two, when they found out about shifters, and it wasn't pretty. You had to hand it to Vivian, though. She was handling this with grace, or maybe it was denial. If Vivian looked a little green around the gills, it was perfectly understandable.

Like Lucius, I suspected what set off this incident. And like Lucius I was ticked. Both Sean and Daniel looked guilty as sin, and damn it, the last thing we needed was complications on this job. Get in, get it done, and move on, was Fire Team Wolf's motto. Daniel and Sean where making sticky complications.

Lucius went on about the danger Vivian was in which didn't help her demeanor or her nerves one bit. I didn't blame her for wanting us out, and I didn't blame her for agreeing to let us stay. This would make it both easier and more difficult. We won't have to make excuses about what we are doing, but in my experience, the principal—that being

Vivian now—will want to be included on every decision. This could slow us down.

"Kyle, take Vivian to her room while I have a chat with Sean and Daniel here."

"Sure, and I'll order us some pizza."

Lucius frowned at me; his temper was painfully short now. Daniel and Sean have been with us long enough to know this was not the circumstance or time of the year to fuck things up.

"Because you'll be busy with these guys and I'll be busy watching Vivian," I said.

"Fine," he growled. Lucius never thought about food when he's upset, which was often lately and especially now, the anniversary of when we were kicked out of our pack. This whole thing with Sean and Daniel wouldn't make things easier.

"Hey, Vivian," I said. "How about letting me in on what's good for pizza around here."

"Pizza." She snorted. "Really. I see two of you shift to wolves, and you want to eat pizza? Like, oh yeah, I just changed into my tee shirt and jeans and I'm down for some Italian."

She walked toward the kitchen, not the upstairs like Lucius ordered, but I followed because the last thing I wanted was to upset her further. With my shifter hearing, I caught that Lucius gave both Daniel and Sean the dressing down of their lives. If they shifted and offered their bellies in submission, I wouldn't be surprised. An Alpha's disapproval carries a lot of weight, even if we are gung-ho grunts that can whup anyone's ass.

Vivian stood by the back door, putting her hands on either side of the glass pane that looked out over the river that flowed by her backyard. Despite the unsightly condition of the house, this was a beautiful plot of land—almost two acres—and there was a pier on the river that needed a little fixing up to be serviceable. Wouldn't it be nice to have a boat here and jaunt down to Long Island Sound and do some fishing?

We moved around so much I don't entertain thoughts like that often, but a homey place like this made you think of what could be.

"So you think you'll sell this house," I asked.

Vivian curled her fingers on the door.

"I don't want to. But Nona left so many bills. The hospital alone—"

"Understandable." I pulled two beers from the fridge and offered her one.

She shook her head. "I don't need anything else to bend my head today."

I winked at her because the way she crinkled her nose was so damned cute. "Maybe you do."

She picked up the phone and dialed a number. "Sal, this is Vivian. Thanks. We'll all miss her. Can you send me three—" she looked at me, and I shook my head "—four pizzas to my house. No, I'm not having a party. I've got some guys here working on the house to get it ready for sale. Yeah, I think I have to. We'll pay by credit card, right?"

I pulled the pack card out of my wallet and handed it to her.

"No, Sal. You don't have to do that. It's the guys who want it. Me? Yeah, I'd love a meatball grinder. You know how I like 'em. Thanks." There was a bit of a pause. "Oh, for heaven's sake," she said with exasperation. "He won't take my, or rather your money."

"We'll give them a huge tip?" I suggested.

"Yeah, I suppose."

I popped the cap for her and pressed the beer in her hand. "Must be nice growing up in a small town where everyone knows you."

"It's good and bad. People always know who you are and where you came from. What was it like for you? Where did you grow up?"

"Northwest, I'm not even sure of the place exactly. It's not like we used human maps. Lucius and I traveled a long time until we got to California. But that time we were tired of living off the land, and picking out ticks from each other's asses, and decided to try the human life. That didn't work out so well seeing we didn't have identification papers. One night we were so desperate for food we landed in an army recruiting station. It was some sort of event night and they served hot dogs and donuts, and we gobbled everything we could.

"How old were you?"

"Late teens, around the age humans graduate from high school. And this guy goes, 'Looks like you need work and regular meals. I can get that for you.' We explained that we didn't have papers, and he said that wasn't a problem and the next thing we knew we were on a bus to Fort Irwin in the Mojave desert."

"How did he work that out. Seems like that would be illegal."

I sighed. "Not unheard of. Done sometimes. But it got us kicked out at the end. Anyway, that's the story of how we landed in the army. Later we applied for the Rangers and then did a few tours. An audit landed us in the stockade, and then they turned us loose."

She bit her lip again, and my insides flipped. I understood now what Daniel and Sean saw in her because she was gorgeous. Not in a movie star kind of way, but as the girl-next-door—a solid woman that could handle the world.

"That sucks," she said. "I'm sure you guys served with distinction. It doesn't seem right."

"There's a whole lot of not right in the world. And if there weren't we wouldn't have jobs."

Lucius stopped yelling, and then the doorbell rang. Vivian ran to the door but Lucius beat her before she could get to it.

"What did I tell you? You are in danger. Always let one of us get the door. Kyle, I told you to take her upstairs."

"You did, Sarg."

"Give the delivery person a fifty," said Vivian. "Then I'll go upstairs."

Lucius grimaced, and pushed Vivian against the wall. Lucius signed for me to get in position, so I did, with my hand on my sidearm at my back ready to draw.

"Pizza," said the driver when Lucius opened the door.

"Yeah, sure. Here you go," said Lucius shoving a Grant in the young man's hands.

"Is Vivian okay," asked the kid.

"Yeah, she's fine."

"I'm fine, Dennis," Vivian said bright standing away from the wall, so the kid could see her. "Now you give that fifty to your dad. This pizza isn't for me."

"Oh, damn. I thought it was a tip."

Lucius grumbled and pulled out a Lincoln. "There. Thanks, Dennis. Bye." Without a word, Lucius shut the door in the kid's face.

"Hey," said Vivian. "I used to babysit that guy. If you don't want to alarm the whole village, you do not upset the pizza delivery guy. His family knows everyone in town."

"Fine," grumbled Lucius. "I'll pen him a letter of apology. "

Vivian grabbed a long, skinny brown bag off the top of the boxes.

"My grinder," she said.

Lucius handed me a box. "Take her upstairs now."

"You're a grouch," snapped Vivian.

I had to keep my guffaws to myself because Vivian was right. She turned and fled up the stairs with me following right after her.

VIVIAN

The only thing that kept me grounded against this insanity was my delicious meatball grinder. It was perfect, with the roll baked toasty and crunchy. Peppers and onions and sauce surround the steaming meatballs and melty mozzarella and provolone cheese spilled over the bun. I'd live for one of these grinders; if I had one of these my last hour on earth, I would die a happy woman.

But death is too good for me, because not only did I run for my life in Colombia, but also boarded a plane and came straight to my hometown. Unknowingly I became party to a vast conspiracy. Men that turn into wolves were all around me, and there was one thing that kept haunting me.

They were all sexy as sin.

I didn't know what this meant. I liked all of them—or rather Sean, Daniel, and Kyle. Lucius was a toss-up, though what woman wouldn't like to get her hands on his sexy pecs. So, I was a little freaked out right now. More than a little. I was so freaked that the only thing that held my sanity was an Italian meatball sandwich—the only normal thing in my life.

Kyle stared at me over his pizza, and damn it, he was

model gorgeous. With his blond hair and caramel brown eyes, he'd make any woman sizzle. Under his gaze, I melted more than the marshmallows Daniel and I made.

Was it any wonder I'm confused? How could I be so turned on by four men at once?

This was insanity, all of it, from Colombia to this minute. And what did Rick give me that someone was willing to kill me for it? I'd only taken a few bites of my grinder, but I found myself obsessed with the idea of finding what Rick could have given me. Where would he put it? I looked around wildly for my backpack and scuttled off my bed where I had sat and looked around for it.

"What's going on Vivian?"

"I need to find my backpack. I'm sure whatever Rick took from though drug lords were in there."

"We've already looked."

"What? You went through my things?"

"When you and Sean went shopping for supplies."

"You went through my things!"

Kyle's expression turned pained, and it made me feel terrible—but no worse than the fact they violated my privacy. It didn't matter that it was for my own good.

"We had to. It was for your own good."

"Yeah, that's right. All you poking and prodding in my stuff, all for my safety. Coming to my house, pretending to be something you weren't."

"Vivian," said Kyle spreading his hands. "Be realistic."

"Realistic? What's realistic about any of this? Werewolves? Colombia drug cartels out to get me? I'm just one archeology student, not important in the broader scheme of things and these things simply do not happen!"

My voice rose as my level of panic did; I was so very, very screwed. Holy hell, I had four werewolves in my house. Little Red Riding Hood had nothing on me.

"Whoa. Sorry. I did not mean to minimize this," Kyle said reasonably raising his hands. Incongruously, his pizza slice hung to the side, the cheese threatening to slide off.

"Watch it," I said moving forward with a napkin the catch the impending greasy mess.

"What?" he said as I got close, and our hands collided, and I accidentally bumped into his chest. Kyle's eyes grew wide as his nostrils flared, and he caught my hand with his.

"Well, hello," he said.

Kyle's scent rose to my nose, an enticing aroma of fresh moss and earth that was entirely *him.* It had me captivated.

He turned the pizza slice to my mouth.

"Do you like pizza?"

"Yes," I said. My throat was dry, and I husked the word out.

"Here," he said. Kyle pushed it closer, and I almost didn't have a choice but to bite down on it.

"Good, huh?"

"Yes." Butterflies fluttered in my stomach. What the hell was I doing? And why was I doing this with Kyle?

Because he's damned handsome.

Kyle drew me in as magnetically as Sean and Daniel, and I was very confused. As I inhaled his musk, I couldn't think about right or wrong or the inevitable complications. The only thing on my mind was kissing his lips.

Reading my mind, Kyle leaned forward and brushed his lips to mine. It was electric, and his lips held red pepper from the pizza that sizzled my flesh.

His shining eyes met mine. In them I saw a man that had found heaven and wanted to explore it. Kyle's large hand curled around my neck, and he pulled me closer to capture my mouth in a deeper kiss. Though his amber stubble scraped my skin, the touch of his lips to mine was eager. In his enthusiasm, there was a tender quality to it, inviting me to take more of him. Without thinking, I opened my mouth to taste this delicious man. His tongue swept the inside of my mouth and then curled around mine; his touch overwhelmed my jumbled mind. All I wanted was to press my body against his. Raw and wild need kindled a fire deep within me; there was nothing else I wanted but him. Our kisses became frantic, and my breathing sped up. I hadn't a clue as to where this would lead, and I didn't want to know, or think but just feel.

Kyle pulled away, and I gasped afraid he would stop.

"Lay back, baby," he said. "Grab onto the headboard."

I did, and wondered what he had in mind as he pushed my tee shirt up and exposed my lacy bra.

"Very nice," he rumbled. "But you won't need that now." He reached behind me to unsnap it, pushing it up to expose my breasts. Like a hungry man he descended on them, sucking in one nipple. He moved just as quickly to the other and my back arched as his warm, wet mouth sent fire through my body. Damn, this man wasn't just hot. He was *explosive.*

I hung onto the headboard, watching him devour my breast as his hard cock pressed to my thigh. I wriggled to try to get into a better position, but he would have none of it. He smiled as he rose and unbuttoned my jeans and pulled them off. Kyle fingered the lacy underwear.

"Should I take these off or not?" he said.

"What are you going to do?" I said, near desperation. Kyle gave me a sly smile.

"Make you scream," he said.

"That's confident of you."

"I have skills." He smirked.

"Such as?"

"You'll see," he said.

He pulled my legs apart and sighed deeply.

"You are incredible," he said as he stroked my inner thigh

with his index finger, sending wild shivers through me. He lowered his head to my thighs and kissed them, swirling his tongue on my sensitive skin. Pleasure shook through me and I squeaked out a small noise. His kisses grew closer to my panties, lapping the silky lace between my legs.

"Goddess, you are delicious," he moaned.

I barely heard him. My hands grasped the headboard tighter as his tongue sought out my most secret places. His soft tongue quested every inch between my legs and my back arched off the bed and one pleasurable jolt after another sizzled through my body. Sizzles turned to fiery heat, each lick and nibble searing my tender flesh as I moaned. Each stroke of his tongue drove me higher beyond sense and reason, and I exploded.

"Kyle!" I cry.

I felt a nip on my inner thigh, and then he continued to lap and kiss me until I pushed his head away. "Sweetie, that's too much."

He smiled sheepishly. "It tasted too good to stop."

Furious knocking on the door had Kyle scrambling to hand me my pants.

"Sarg wants to see you downstairs *now*."

"Oops," said Kyle.

"Oops?" I said. "Is there something wrong?"

"No," said Kyle with a frown. "I just have to straighten a few things out with these guys. You get some rest." He winked at me and then left the room, barely opening the door to scoot through.

I heard some harsh words outside the door before Kyle let out a roar.

"Just leave her alone. She's been through enough."

I wasn't a shy flower that needed the big bad wolf to take care of me, so I pulled on my slacks. Before I pulled them over my hips I see there was a black and blue mark on my inner thigh. Kyle did that. When I looked closer I swore I could see teeth marks. What the hell? Kyle did that? I barely felt anything.

Loud voices came up the stairwell and the heat vent by my bed. I didn't know what was going on in my house, but I was going to find out.

LUCIUS

I couldn't believe these guys. Sean and Daniel? Outrageous. I should kick their butts from one end of the continent to the other, for revealing us as shifters to Vivian. The last thing we needed is humans—any human for that matter—to know about us. What the hell were they thinking?

And Kyle? He's the guy I expected to have my back, but you couldn't get around shifter hearing. I knew what he did with Vivian, the woman we were supposed to protect.

I'd never seen my pack act like this, disobeying orders and acting like they were without discipline. I'd worked with these guy for seven years, Kyle twelve, and there was no way that I would expect them to act like teenagers on a co-ed sleepover.

Intolerable.

Sean and Daniel were on clean-up detail in the kitchen, and now I have to speak to Kyle. But instead of coming into the living room, he heads into the kitchen. He knew damn well where I was, and he ignored me.

I would kick his shifter ass.

"Way to go, brah," said Sean. "You were supposed to protect her, not—"

"Shut up," said Kyle angrily and uncharacteristically. "Don't talk that way about my mate."

"Your mate?" growled Sean.

"Yeah, *your* mate?" snapped Daniel.

It looked like the whole pack was rearing to go at it again; I wouldn't have that.

"What the hell?" I huffed. "What are you all going on about? There is no way that one woman is the mate to all of you."

"What do you mean—mate?" said a feminine voice.

I whipped my head to see Vivian standing in the doorway.

This was going from bad to worse.

"Vivian, you should go to your room."

"Look, Mr. Alpha, I don't know who you think you are, but you are not my father and have zero right to tell me what to do. In fact, I want all of you to clear out."

"No can do," I said as I narrowed my eyes. "Fire Team Wolf does not leave a job half done."

"Kyle does," sniggered Daniel.

"Shut it," snapped Kyle irritably.

"Quit it!" I commanded. "Daniel, go patrol north, Sean south, and I swear to the Goddess if you get in each other's way, I'll take a chunk out of your hides myself. Go!"

Sean and Daniel gave sidelong glances at Vivian but did what they were told, which was good; I was fast losing patience with them.

"You want me to—"

"No. Because we've got to get to the bottom of this. And since your pops was the pack shaman, I figure you know a few bits to get a handle on this. You know, like that stuff you fed Aleesha and me before we all took off."

"What the hell are you talking about?" said Vivian.

"I told you we left," Kyle said. "But I didn't tell you why. Lucius was in love with the Alpha's daughter. The old man announced a mating agreement with his daughter and another pack's Alpha. Lucius asked me if there was any way to break the agreement, and from what my father said, the only way was with a *sacred bond* crafted by the moon goddess, usually with more than one male to make a sacred pact to defend against an immense evil. The thinking is that such a pack was stronger and could overcome great obstacles."

Vivian cast a suspicious glance at each of us.

"That sounds like a load of BS."

"It would, normally," I said. "But the thing is we are a pack of four facing an unknown number enemies. They are vicious, without mercy and can strike without warning."

"Yeah," said Kyle. "Perhaps this whole situation has kicked up a new bunch of instincts. Protecting you is our first mission, and a wolf is never as protective than when he protects his mate."

"It could be." I said. "The old stories of such things were the responses to the same situation."

"Well, that's just great," said Vivian with her hands on her hips. "I've got a bunch of horny wolves after me because I spark their protective instincts? Yeah. Not going to work. You fellas need to leave."

Vivian and I faced off. "Go get Sean and Daniel. We need to talk."

Kyle knew better than disobey a direct order, but he hesitated, looking to me, then Vivian and back to me again.

"What are you going to do, Sarg?"

"I don't answer to you. Hop to it, Corporal."

"Yes, Sir," he said unhappily. "You need anything, Vivian —call."

"Go!" I put enough force in my words that Kyle moved

toward the door without another word. The door shut with a hard thud, so I knew he was ticked.

Screw him.

"What are you going to do Mr. Big, Bad Wolf? Protect me against my will?" Vivian stood before me with her delicate hands on the doorframe staring up at me fiercely with those beautiful melty brown eyes of hers, the color of milk chocolate shining with shots of warm copper. Funny, I hadn't noticed until now how the light glinted off them like a doe's eyes when she's about to take flight into the forest. A growl rumbled through my chest as my wolf sees the thing I had ignored.

Mate.

Fuck, it was happening to me too.

"If I have to. I preferred we get along."

Vivian's mouth formed a hard line as she stared at me. One hand gripped the door frame while the other fell to her side as if she would use it as leverage to turn and run. Her chest rose and fell; I couldn't help but notice the swell of her breasts between the v of her white tee shirt.

My wolf wailed and chaffed inside of me, desperate to get out, to *touch* this woman. Think of a puppy scratching the door to get outside, then transpose that to two hundred pounds of teeth, fur, claws and muscle and you'd get an idea of the beast that raged inside me. I was no pup that couldn't control his changes, but her scent rolled off her, and my self-control hung by a thread.

She released the door jam and faced me.

"What makes you think that you can order me around?" Her defiant voice snapped my self-control. My wolf surged forward, and I managed to hold it back by inches. Still, my heart pounded and my wolf snarled, ready to take down this challenge to my authority.

"You better go up to your room, Vivian," I said coldly. If she didn't back away, then things would go too far.

"And if I don't?"

That was it. I strode forward and swept her into my arms and jaunted up the steps two at a time. Her eyes got very wide, but I moved so quickly she understood things could go badly.

"Stop," she protested.

I kicked in the door to her bedroom, and damn if I didn't splinter the middle panel. Home repairs were last on my list now. I lay her on her bed, though I didn't move my hands from her shoulders or her bottom. In fact, her bum felt hot and welcoming, and I didn't want to walk away.

She stared at me with wide, blown pupils. Her heart beat rapidly like a bird in flight. What should have been fear was anything but; arousal wafted between us, calling me. I was the alpha, and she was my mate, and she *was* going to understand that.

With a jolt, I stepped back. This was wrong. I couldn't let my wolf get the best of me.

"Lucius," said Vivian. She held up her hand to me. "Don't go."

I closed my eyes, but my wolf, damn him is doing a happy dance inside me. I took her hand and felt the beat of her pulse from its palm.

"If I stay," I rumbled, "I won't be leaving. That's how it works among my kind, not with mates."

"But that other girl—"

"I was young and not as strong as I am now. No one can best me like that again."

She pulled me closer, so I stand at the edge of the bed.

"I agree this is all craziness, Lucius but it's hard to understand how this is all happening so quickly."

The world spun out of control, and fire burned through

me like I'd never known before. I pressed one knee into the mattress and gathered her into my arms. Our lips touched, as sweet as summer fruit, wet and filled with heat. I pushed her over gently and lay down next to her, but in the next second turned her to lay on to top of me. I was hard as a rock and I saw the desire in her eyes.

In a move unlike me, I threw caution to the wind.

DANIEL

I wanted to run, far and long through the state park I saw on the map and get lost in the undergrowth of nature, listening to birds and sniffing for prey. Above all, I wanted to be rid of this impossible situation where each of my pack mates crawled over my mate like it was their right. Angry at everyone, all I could do was walk circular paths on the cut lawn that ran into a dark green boxwood hedge that lined the front of the property and cut a sharp turn to travel the northern property line until it ran to the river. Almost two acres away Sean did the same thing on the southern property border.

Just like Lucius to kick us out of the house to get us out of the way. I didn't want to think of what he was doing with Vivian. He had that look in his eye as if he wanted her. Hell, my whole pack wanted my mate, and I railed against the unfairness of this.

Patrol north, I groused as I followed the hedge line up and down the perimeter. The sticky August humidity wasn't helped by the sun sinking toward the tree line far across the road that passed by Vivian's house. A light breeze wafted from the river lacking the promise of relief. A few houses over a dog barked, and a car horn sounded, and farther away an ambulance siren wailed through the streets. It was a normal American town, normal not being what we were used to.

But it was nice.

This was a gorgeous piece of property. It would be a shame for Vivian to give it up. This was a great place to raise a family.

Whoa, soldier. Where did that idea come from?

Mate? Right? rumbled my wolf.

This guy already got me in trouble with my pack mates *and* my Alpha, and now he wanted to push me toward fatherhood? How did that work anyway? I mean, she was human and I *definitely* was not. How in heck would she handle if the kids took after dear old dad, and changed from pup to human on a whim? Pups weren't known for their self-control, and you certainly couldn't have the neighborhood kids over to play if Danny Jr. wolfed out at the slightest provocation.

My head spun, thinking of building a life with Vivian; I didn't know which way was up.

I was raised in a human foster family, but that started at the age of ten when my pack was decimated in a pack war. Truth be told I never got over being the sole survivor of the slaughter, and in my heart of hearts, all I wanted was a family of my own. Until now, I thought the pack was it.

I heard footsteps through the grass and from the gait, I knew it is Kyle.

"What the hell do you want?" I growled.

"Relax, I just came to talk to you."

"Take your comedy act on the road. I'm not interested."

"Look, jerk, this is important. Because it involves all of us, including Vivian."

"Like I said," I snarled. Anger curled in my gut and if he didn't get away from me, my fist would meet his jaw. By the look on Kyle's face, he had the same thought.

I couldn't help it. The holier-than-thou smug look in his eyes lit something in my primal brain, and I smashed an upper cut into his jaw. Kyle stumbled back, grunting as he held his jaw with his hand. A second later, he charged me and knocked me over. We rolled around on the ground trying to get a shot into each other, but both of us were too good. We blocked each other's shots and grappled like two school kids trying and failing to beat the hell out of the other.

Finally, Kyle managed to sit on my stomach and held my shoulders with his hands while I snarled at him.

"What the fuck, Daniel?"

"You stay away from me. I have nothing to say to you, Sean, or Lucius."

Kyle shook his head.

"I get that this is difficult, but you need to listen."

Yeah, right. Like I was going to listen to someone that betrayed me. Yes, betrayal, because that's what it was. In the history of mankind, only one kind of man moved in on his brother's woman. A rat. A Judas. A Judas Rat. That's what I'll call him. Like they call me F.K., I'll call him J.R.

Kyle stared at me waiting for me to say something. Okay. I did.

"You going to make me?"

"What are you? Eight years old? Holy Goddess, Daniel, we need to talk about this like adults."

"I don't need to do shit, except maybe leave this pack."

"Leave the pack?" he scoffed. "That's not going to help you. Because none of us are going anywhere."

"I'll make sure of it."

"You think you can out alpha Lucius?"

"I'll give it a good try."

Kyle shook his head. "Buddy, you are not thinking clearly, but I understand it. Vivian has gotten under all our skins. Face it. All our wolves think of her as our mate."

"That can't be possible," I objected.

"It is. It's rare enough, but it is. If one woman arouses the protective instinct of the pack, then the whole pack takes her as a mate."

"No," I scoffed.

Kyle nodded. "There are old stories my dad told in his role as pack shaman. It seemed to happen when a great evil befell the land and all that mythic stuff. And Lucius and I think that is what happened here. The threat of the cartel, and us spending time in her home and perhaps even taking care of her house, switched on some ancient instincts."

My fists curled in my hand. "That doesn't seem right. My wolf doesn't like it."

"Neither does mine, but we're a pack. We've shared all sorts of things. Remember those girls in Okinawa?"

I do. It was a fun, no-holds-barred weekend.

"Oh, man, that was wild—but that was for play. This is like, for life."

"I know. It's some serious shit. But I don't know about your wolf, but mine will be miserable if we don't give this a try."

Mate.

Oh hell. My wolf whined for her. It would be miserable to walk away from her.

"What was it like when you and Lucius shared—"

Kyle gave me a cutting glance.

"Seriously, you are asking me about that?"

"You've done it before."

Kyle rubbed the back of his neck looking very embarrassed.

"It was more of a concept than a thing. Aleesha's father

caught up to us before we could, you know, seal the deal. Brah, it was a raw part of our lives, teenagers trying to be adults."

"I can understand that," I said. We all have parts of our younger years that we'd rather forget. Missteps, clumsy moments, outright stupidity. Kyle and Lucius, according to their accounts, were too young to form a lifetime union with anyone.

"But sometimes, you know, I miss her. And I know Lucius does. I think it's time that we connect with another woman. Aleesha seems now more like a dream than something that could have been."

I blew out a long breath. This idea, all of us sharing Vivian was a little more than I can handle. Even in my dim memories of my pack no one ever shared a mate.

"I don't know."

Kyle scoffed. "If there is one trait that defines us shifters, it's stubbornness."

"I am not stubborn," I protested.

"Says the man arguing with me."

I have to admit he has a point. "This is a great discussion, but there is one person who opinion counts more than anyone else's."

"Yeah?"

"Vivian. She wasn't raised like you, Lucius, or me. How can you be sure she's going to go along with it?

Kyle shrugged his shoulders. "Lucius is talking with her now."

"Talking!" I spit. "How can you be sure they are only talking?"

"You have a point. We need to get Sean on board right now."

SEAN

We were out on a Ranger training mission, the mountain section, and by this point, I was pretty hungry. After the initial training period of short rations, all of us were. But Lucius took Daniel and me off for 'special training,' and since he was the instructor, of course, we went. Kyle stayed with, or so we thought, the rest of the unit.

Lucius built a fire, and we sat around it. Daniel and I passed looks wondering what would happen next. Our stomachs grumbled, and Lucius scowled like he usually did, while he sharpened a stick. He didn't tell us to do the same, so we just sat there.

"You hungry, men?" he asked.

"Yeah, Sarg," I said.

"Thought so. Short rations are supposed to train you up to hardship, but there is nothing in the rules that say we can't eat off the land."

"How are we supposed to do that, Sarg?" said Daniel.

"Come on," said Lucius disparagingly. "Don't tell me that neither of you has noticed that you see better at night than the others in your unit."

"Sure," said Daniel. "But that doesn't mean anything."

"Doesn't it? And what do you smell? Around you?"

Daniel's nose crinkled. "Something dead."

"So right," said Lucius with a smile. "Chuck the first one," he called.

A brown furry thing flew in the air and landed by the fire and Lucius picked it up. It was a rabbit, with its head hanging limply. He tossed it to Daniel.

"Clean that," he ordered. "Now the others."

Two more dead rabbits flew through the night, and Lucius tossed one to me.

"I suspect Daniel remembers how to do this, but you, City Boy, never got the chance."

I puckered my lips looking at it. I'd rather eat an MRE than this thing.

"You never have to go hungry in the wild, not with your native abilities."

"Where did this come from?"

"Kyle, you can come out now."

We both turned our heads toward the darkened woods when two yellow eyes glowed at us. A gray wolf stepped forward, its yellow fangs bared and stained with blood.

"That's not him," I said, scrambling backward.

"Sure it is. Kyle, come into the circle."

The wolf stepped out of the darkness, snarling at us with menace.

"Fuck," I yelled.

"Okay, corporal, you can stop gaslighting the privates, now."

Kyle shifted, laughing his head off, standing there naked. Lucius tossed him a pair of camos, and I fainted.

I never lived that moment down. Whenever I hung back, my pack reminded me of that moment when I just lost it. I never have since, because the ribbing I took after was a good enough reminder.

So, when Lucius shifted that night, I didn't faint though I did feel sick. Between the blood on my hands from inexpertly cleaning the rabbit, my exhaustion and hunger from training, I felt like I'd chuck my cookies. Lucius growling at me in wolf form—that would not go over big.

And then Kyle told Daniel to shift, and he said he didn't remember. The bastard knew all along he was a shifter. When Lucius attacked Daniel to force it out of him, I watched in amazement as Daniel changed from human to wolf, destroying a good pair of fatigues.

That was the night I learned the truth about all of us. I didn't shift that night, but I did eat roasted rabbit—which by the way wasn't too bad. Later, as I grew more used to my wolf form, meals were not so civilized.

It took me a while to wrap my head around all this, but I did, at least when it came to shifting and running with my pack. But the rest of it?

I didn't have memories of pack life like Kyle does. I wasn't raised in a shifter pack like Lucius and Kyle. The things that came naturally to them, obedience to the Alpha, the pecking order of the pack, working in unison with each other, is kind of like the military, but not really. Whereas in the service you eventually go home and kick up your feet, we live pack discipline twenty-four seven. Raised human, this wolf stuff seemed surreal at times. I hadn't minded so much until I met Vivian.

With Vivian, I wanted to be with her, without the others around.

I knew that Lucius was the boss, but I didn't like for a second that he was alone with Vivian in the house. And Kyle? I wanted to tear his head off his shoulders. What was he thinking going near her? I scented her on him when he walked into the kitchen, and if Lucius weren't standing right there, I would have.

This was all very confusing because I loved all these guys like brothers. We were tight, and you can even say the old bros before—well, you know what I mean. The pack came first. Or it should.

I didn't anymore.

I heard a whistle, and I knew it was Kyle. Well, I wasn't letting him call me like some dog. He may be the Beta of the pack, but he's not my Alpha. I double timed my steps to put some distance between us.

"Hey, Sean. Slow down."

"Fuck off."

"Sean," said Daniel. "Hold up. You're supposed to be patrolling the perimeter, not going for a run."

"I want to see you less than him," I snapped over my shoulder.

Kyle caught up to me and spun me around.

"Stop. Just stop. There are things you do not understand."

"Yeah? You've been telling me that for five years, and I'm tired of hearing it. You had no business putting your hands on my mate."

"And what makes you think she's yours? Eh?"

"My wolf says so."

"So now your wolf is talking to you? You said he didn't."

"Apparently when something is important he does."

"That's nice for you. But you still can't run off and act like a lone wolf. You're part of this pack."

"Maybe I shouldn't be if my pack mates can't respect what's mine."

"*Dude,*" said Daniel coming up being Kyle. "You've got this all wrong. Vivian is not a possession. Talking about a human woman like she is will get you in trouble."

"Like you would know." I was thoroughly unreasonable,

and a part of me knew it. There was another part of me that wanted to pound these guys into the ground. I weighed my options here as well as different martial arts moves. Though I know these guys fight as well as me, I might be able to surprise them and get in first licks.

"Granted, none of us has done the girlfriend thing in quite a while, let alone consider a woman a mate," said Kyle. "But here's the thing. I don't think she's your mate."

"Now wait a minute," I growled. Or my wolf did. All I knew was that I didn't like the words coming out of his mouth.

"Now hold on and listen. I think she is our mate—all of ours."

"All?" I said. The idea hit me like a hammer, and I stepped back. "That can't be right."

"According to Kyle and his shaman father, yeah, it can," said Daniel.

Mind officially blown. Vivian belonged to all of us.

"Well, how's that supposed to work out? "

"Don't know," said Daniel.

"We'll have to find a way to work it out," said Kyle. "But there is one thing for sure. We aren't going to do that out here."

"Let's go talk to Vivian," I said.

I didn't know what to expect when we all filed into the house. Lucius and Vivian weren't in the kitchen, the living room or the dining room. We all heard moans coming from Vivian's room.

"That's just great," said Sean.

Daniel gave a low growl in his throat.

"There is only way to handle this," I said. "Come on, men."

I did not know if they would follow me, but before any of this went any farther, we were going to get some things straight.

At Vivian's door, I knocked. Daniel and Sean crowded behind me.

"Everyone decent in there?"

"Go away, Kyle," grumbled Lucius.

"I'm just telling you if there is anything you don't want us to see, get it covered up."

"I told you," said an entirely displeased Lucius.

"One—" I said.

"Don't you dare."

"Two—"

"I swear."

"Three. Coming in Lucius. Don't say I didn't warn you."

"What happened to the door?" said Sean.

"Hurricane Lucius," muttered Daniel.

"I like that," I said. "We should call him Hurricane."

"Sure," said Daniel doubtfully.

I swung open the door and found Lucius sitting bare chested on the bed, with Vivian, obviously naked under her comforter. Her checks were flushed, and there was a blush across the top of her breasts.

"What are you people doing?" growled Lucius.

"We figured we should talk with Vivian and clue her in on what's going on, seeing that you, um, got distracted."

"Who says I got distracted?"

"Your lack of a shirt for one thing."

Daniel rounded the further side of the bed and sat down next to her and slipped his arm behind her neck.

"Hi, babe."

Sean sat on the opposite side.

"Hi, darling," he said with a big smile.

I decided to sit in the middle, and the bed dipped. I stare into her warm brown eyes.

"Hi, sweetheart."

"Kyle," grumbled Lucius. "I swear to the Goddess if you don't get out of here—"

"You know what's happening, Lucius. You can't Alpha your way out of this one. Vivian, you remember what we said about us as a pack."

"There was some craziness about all you thinking I'm your mate?"

"Yes," I said in my smoothest voice. "There is nothing more definite for a shifter as when he recognizes her."

"It sounds crazy to me," she said.

"The craziest part is that all of our wolves think of you as our mate. And it's not usual, especially with a human woman, but we can't argue with our essential natures." I looked over my shoulder to Lucius. "How am I doing, Sarg?"

"Okay," he grumbled.

"You'll get used to that," I said to Vivian. "He's always been a grouchy bastard."

"What if I don't want to get used to it? Hell, I've dated only a handful of guys, let alone four at once."

"It wouldn't be dating, babe," said Daniel. "More like having four husbands."

"Four husbands! Now that is crazy."

"I agree," said Sean. "It sounds like a little much. But you'd never lack for company."

"We can't exactly promise that," said Lucius. "We do have to work."

"That's fine with me," said Vivian. "I have this little thing called an education to attend to. I don't have time for four husbands."

"Mates," I said gently. "And you can do whatever you like. We have plenty of money."

"Great," complained Lucius. "Now you get free with the cash."

"She's our mate, Lucius. She can have anything she wants."

"Yes, she can," said Daniel as he kissed her temple. "Um, yum."

"My what big eyes you have," said Vivian turning her face to his. He leaned in and kissed her. "That's not the only thing I have that's big," he said when he broke away.

"Smooth, brah," said Sean rolling his eyes.

"You're not feeling left out?" said Vivian to Sean.

"Not yet," he said. Then Sean leaned in smothered her mouth with a kiss. When he pulled away Vivian's eyes turned wide.

"I couldn't pick one of you."

"That's the idea," I said. "We don't want you to."

"Still," she said. "I want, no I need, to see you as your other selves."

That brought a smile to my lips.

"What you say, Lucius?" I asked.

"She should know what she's getting into."

"Okay then, we'll have to strip," I said to Vivian with a smile. "Clothes can get expensive if we don't."

"Uh huh, there's always a catch, isn't there?" Her eyes held a mischievous glint.

I chuckled and pulled off my tee-sheet and tossed it over my shoulder.

"It's not a damn strip show," complained Daniel.

"Maybe I like strip shows," said Vivian. "What are you guys waiting for? Show me what you boys have."

"I like your attitude," I said with a wink. After all these years it didn't take me long to shift. Of course, Lucius wouldn't let me outdo him. Before I knew it, he had his clothes off.

Vivian stared as his body morphed into his black wolf. He'd done it so long, his human arms and legs changed shape with ease. Shoulders realigned, and his muzzle elongated. Normal human ears shifted from the side to the top of his head, all within a blink of an eye.

Vivian stared, her face frozen in an unreadable expression, and I was afraid that watching Lucius' transformation was too much and that she'd lose it. But her face softened.

"You're beautiful," Vivian said in awe.

He barked and jumped on the bed and knocking Sean and Daniel off because he's that big. Lucius nuzzled her face, and she laughed.

I shifted next, and finally, Sean and Daniel got into the act, and we were all scrambling to find a place on the bed with her in a tumult of competition between us trying to get in licks on her face.

"Whoa!" she laughed. Daniel worked at pulling her comforter down with it clamped between his teeth, shaking his head, while she held onto it fiercely as she giggled and protested. A flurry of muzzles nuzzled her in every place possible, and she kicked and thrashed laughing and I realized she was ticklish.

Now that was something to work with. Lucius realized it too, and shifted to sit between her legs.

"Seen enough, gorgeous?" he said.

"I'm not sure. You guys sure are playful as wolves."

"I don't know about these other guys, but I don't play."

*L*ucius' deep, rich voice made me shiver. His eyes burned into my soul and I felt as if we were connected. You would think that such a rough warrior wouldn't know tenderness, but you would be wrong. We spent the time we had before Kyle, Daniel and Sean entered in long, slow kisses and caresses that set every one of my nerve endings ablaze. He hadn't been in a hurry, and I found that amazing and our lovemaking brought me to the verge of begging for more when Kyle, Daniel and Sean entered.

I was surrounded by four handsome, intriguing men —*shifter men*—all of whom wanted me. They filled my bed, naked. If you think that having one ripped and toned man in your bedroom is great, think four. It was like Christmas day had come and I'd hit the lottery too.

They were all buff as if they spent days upon days in the gym, but they were different too. Lucius with his hair clipped to a dark shadow had the most muscly chest, and his thighs were beefy. Kyle was only a bit shorter than Lucius but his blond hair and brown melted chocolate eyes made him a delectable treat. My eyes flick to his cock, thick and long; I can't help wonder what it tastes like.

Sandy-haired Daniel was two hundred pounds of lean muscle and his eyes, though not as piecing green as Lucius', blazed with passion. Sean's deep brown hair was almost black until it caught glints of sunlight—only further lighting up his blue eyes. They were all big men, but I was drunk with the thought they were all mine.

It was an embarrassment of riches, and though I might expect to feel overwhelmed; I wasn't. I was excited.

"Someone better kiss me," I said.

"Come here," said Lucius.

His large hand took my face and cupped it gently. "Such a perfect mouth needs plenty of kissing." He pressed his lips to mine hungrily, sending tremors of desire through my body. The need he had awakened before the rest of the pack entered came roaring back. Lucius pulled away and swung me around to lay against his muscled chest. The shifter's hard cock pressed against my tailbone and between the cheeks of my ass, sparking tingles of desire.

"Baby," I said trying to turn around to get more of him.

"Shh," Lucius said nibbling my neck. "I'm here, and I'm not going anywhere, but your other mates want you too."

"I never—I don't know how with all of you."

"Sweetheart," said Daniel as he pulled apart my legs. "We'll take this one step at a time, as much or as little as you like."

"That's right," said Kyle moving to lay on my left. He cupped my breast and then lightly stroked it.

"Absolutely," said Sean who took the position on my right. He sucked on my nipple and lapped it with his tongue, and I whimpered.

"That's right, sweetheart," said Daniel. "I love your noises." Daniel bent his head and kissed my thighs, though he growled when his lips hit the mark Kyle left earlier. He licked and nibbled my tender skin murmuring how soft it was, how sweet I tasted until his tongue lashed my folds. With a moan, I arched my back, but Lucius held me fast, and Daniel drove his tongue inside me. I murmured things like baby, so good and more and Daniel obliged me. I was on fire, his touches and kisses all over was a velvet carpet of pleasure that had me squirming.

"Please," I whimpered, though I hardly know what I'm begging for. Sean took my hand and wrapped it around his cock, and the steel within the silk of his skin drove me wild.

"That's it's, darling," he murmured as he wrapped his hands around mine. "You're so fucking hot. I love your touch."

Kyle straddled my waist and pressed my breasts around his cock.

"Oh fuck," he said as he jutted his hips.

Daniel kept hitting the right spots between my legs, and I was overwhelmed. A cock in one hand, and another between my breasts, and a man giving me just the right kind of tongue lashing; I cannot take this. Lucius pulled back my head by my hair, and devoured my mouth with a kiss full of fire and lust, his tongue lashing mine. Sean spilled into my hand with a cry and Kyle called my name as his cum coated the crevice of my breasts. I drowned in all these sensations, going under farther and farther, my heart racing and barely able to breathe. I was on the cusp as Daniel sucked on my clit hard. Pleasure ripped through me like a thousand stars exploding.

Kyle tumbled off me and propped his head on his hand while Sean cleans off my hand. Behind me, Lucius was harder than ever, and he moved his hips slightly. Another ripple of pleasure flowed through me; I wanted more, so much more.

"Baby," I said to Daniel. "I owe you a favor."

"No, hon. You don't owe me a thing,"

"But what if I want to."

"I wouldn't say no."

"Go lay by the headboard," said Lucius to Daniel.

Daniel laid back, and his shaft sticks up hard and long. I licked my lips.

"Let me help you," said Lucius. He put his hands under my arms and helped me to sit up.

"You okay?"

"Oh, yeah," I said a bit dreamily.

He kissed me.

"Let me help you to your knees."

I looked over and saw a glint in his eyes.

"What is your evil plan?"

"Oh, it's not evil at all. But I have been waiting for you."

"I have a date with Daniel."

"I know that. Go ahead." Lucius gave a nod of his head, and I leaned forward and looked into Daniel's eyes, and he smiled. Keeping our gazes locked touched my tongue to the tip of his cock. His taste burst on it, heady and potent. I wanted all of it.

"So good," he said.

I swirled my tongue on the fat tip, and he moaned. Wrapping one hand around the base of his shaft, I licked the underside.

"That's hot," Sean whispered.

"You're telling me," Kyle said. I glanced over my shoulder to see Kyle wrapping his hand around his cock. Oh damn, these guys were hot. Encouraged, I took Daniel into my mouth as far as I could while I stroked his balls.

Then I feel fingers touch my folds stroking it. Lucius leaned over my back and whispered into my ear.

"You're so wet, babe, waiting for me. I need you, need to be inside you."

I lifted my head a moment. "Lucius," I breathed. "I need you too."

He kissed my neck and back.

"Sweet, sweet, Vivian." He pressed his cock at my opening; it felt so *big*. I didn't know if I could take it. Lucius eased in slowly as I sucked on Daniel's cock enjoying the eroticism of this racy moment—a man in my mouth and a man entering me. I moaned around Daniel.

"Oh fuck," he said. "Sweetheart, oh damn." He pushed at my shoulders, and I stopped, not sure of what he wanted. Daniel took his cock and with a few hard tugs painted my chest with his cum.

Lucius grabbed my hips and dove deep inside me and I gasped. Yes, he was big, but he filled me, and each stroke brought pleasure that cannot be described. His cock seared me like a glowing blade of fire, and I push against him as he pummeled me with it.

"Mine," he growled, and his mouth landed on my shoulder and his teeth clamped down. Pain mingled with pleasure as wave after wave of heat pummeled me, until a tsunami of white fire shattered me, and I fell gasping into Daniel's arms.

My pack and my mate sat bedraggled and exhausted at the kitchen table—all of them too tired to make coffee. Last night drained us all; it seemed as if we couldn't get our fill of our mate. Finally, her exhaustion stayed us, and as much as we all wanted to sleep with her, only one of us fit in the bed comfortably.

Last night that was me. Being Alpha had its perks.

My pack mates left the room, but not without extracting promises that I share the wealth on future nights. What else could I say? I am not a selfish Alpha.

We would have to get a bigger bed—maybe custom make one. We'll see. This whole domestic scene would take getting used to, and I could see it was Vivian who would have to make the biggest adjustment. Human and raised as an only child she truly had no idea of what it meant to live with a group of people. And four mates? Definitely more than a human or shifter woman was used to.

Still, I was proud of Vivian for accepting us all. It would have been a dark time if she rejected any of us. And now, we had to do our jobs and protect her.

"Anyone patrol the perimeter this morning?"

Sideways glances to each other told me no.

"I see. And how do we protect Vivian if we don't keep an eye out?"

"I'll go," said Kyle. "Maybe you can send Sean out for some eats and coffee. The cupboard is bare."

"Wait," said Vivian. "Isn't that another fairy tale?"

Daniel groaned. "That is a bad joke."

"Yeah," said Sean brightening. "Because you know what we call Daniel right?"

"No."

"His last name is Oberon. So, we call him F.K. For fairy king."

"Oh," said Vivian with a grimace. "That's bad. And what do they call you, Kyle?"

"Late for dinner," said Sean.

"Har, har," said Kyle sarcastically.

"Let's all go out. I can see from the quality of the jokes that you all need a fill-up. That double wide truck will fit us, all right? That's why we are paying a godawful amount of money for it?"

"You worrying about money, Sarg?"

"Well, I haven't heard from Robbins, and he hasn't paid the balance."

"We're fine," said Kyle. "I'll just move some money around."

"And now all of a sudden you've become Mr. Fast-And-Loose with the cash."

"Didn't we have this discussion? We have a mate now, and we have to make sure things are covered. So, there are some things I want to talk to the group about."

As it turned out, the vehicle for being a monster did not fit us comfortably, so we ended up taking our bikes though Sean insisted on taking Vivian in the truck for safety reasons.

We were treating Vivian like a doll that could break and a shadow crossed Vivian's face when she climbed into the truck.

Kyle, for being a cheap bastard, was good with the money. He had us sitting good with stocks and liquid assets, the last being good for a roving band of shifters. So, when he suggested that we take care of Vivian's outstanding bills as we waited for the waitress, I wasn't surprised. It would eat up some cash, but if it meant taking care of Vivian I was in. So were Daniel and Sean.

It was Vivian that objected.

"I can't have you paying off my bills."

"Of course we will. We're responsible for you," I said this matter-of-factly, but she didn't seem to understand.

"Now wait a minute, big boy. I take care of my own business."

"And you can. No one is stopping you," said Kyle. "But we're part of your life now, and what affects you, affects us. And if you have debt, then we have debt."

"That's right, Viv," said Sean taking her hand. "It ain't a thing. We've been working so long for so hard, that despite what closefisted Kyle says, we've more money than we need."

"That's right," agreed Kyle." And our job calendars fill up quickly. We turn down three jobs a day."

"You do?"

"Sure," said Kyle.

"We do?" I growled. "What has Kyle been hiding from me?

"Don't start, Lucius," said Kyle. "We work 24-7 as it is."

"I'm not sure," said Vivian as she stared into her coffee. "It doesn't seem right."

"No, babe," said Daniel slipping his arm around her shoulder. "What's not right is you thinking that you are on your own. You're not. You are part of us, part of our pack."

"But I'm no wolf."

"Did you ever here the story of Romeo, the Alaskan wolf?" said Sean.

"No."

"Romeo was a wild wolf who would come out of the woods and play with local dogs. He showed up every morning before people took their dogs out for walks. Eventually, most of the townspeople came to trust him, and let him frolic with their pets."

"Yeah," said Daniel. "We understand Romeo. He was probably a lone wolf, who either lost his pack or got kicked out of it. Not finding another wolf pack to join he adopted some dogs as his de facto pack."

"I still don't understand," said Vivian.

"What they are saying, Vivian," I interjected, "is that you don't have to be a wolf to join a wolf pack. Granted our arrangement is unusual in many ways, but since our wolves, all of them, say you belong to us, then you do."

"That's just so incredible."

"There is some that talk about imprinting," said Kyle. He stared thoughtfully into his coffee. "Human babies do it when they are born. Humans call it bonding. And something similar happens when people fall in love."

"Yeah," said Daniel with a smirk. "It's all very chemical."

"Neurochemicals," snorted Sean.

"Mr. Vocabulary there," said Daniel derisively.

"Just because I like to read—"

Kyle scoffed. "You two. Anyway, Viv, in pack life it happens between mates, only we call it fated mates."

"You imprinted on all of us," I said. "So, it's settled."

Vivian looked away, and I watched as the wheels within her mind turned.

"Don't I get a say?"

"Sure," said Daniel with a leer. "Which one you want to be with at any given time."

"You are not helping," said Kyle.

"Don't listen to those jerks," said Sean putting his arm around her. "You do what you want. Just don't expect for us to stay away from you for long."

"I'm not sure, is that good or bad," she said. Vivian pulled away from Sean.

"This," I said, "is new for all of us. We won't crowd you, but until we are sure the threat of the cartel is gone, we will protect you."

"Yeah," said Kyle. "Whether or not we get paid."

Perfect, I thought. *So like Kyle to put money into the equation. Just what the woman needs.*

"I tell you," said Vivian. "Every one of you is wonderful. But I'm used to being a lone wolf. At the moment all of us being together sounded great, but now in the light of day..." She trailed off and stared at her hands

What's her problem? Doesn't she like us? My wolf growled not so much in word but emotions. I glanced at the faces of my pack and saw a similar reaction. This could get ugly fast. Not that we'd hurt her, but when our wolfish emotions get riled we'll take it out on each other. I couldn't let this happen.

"Vivian," I said. "Walk with me. You guys: order up some good eats."

I stood behind Vivian's chair and pulled it out for her and took her hand. Trepidation lined her eyes, but I smiled at her. She followed as I led her to the back entrance and took her out onto a patio with several picnic tables.

"It's too much for you, isn't it?" I said. "The four of us."

She looked away. "I sat at the kitchen table this morning. Kyle, then Daniel, and then Sean showed up and sat looking at me as if I were something to gobble up, and I had a holy shit moment. And then you showed up filling up the doorway, and I lost it. It hit me that I had sex with four men in one night. I'm not that kind of woman, Lucius. I thought if I was lucky, someday I'd meet one nice man, settle down, have the white picket fence and the dog and the 2.4 kids, you know, normal stuff."

"And this isn't normal."

"Four men. Not as husbands, but as mates. At least with a human man, you could get a divorce. Not that anyone has that goal in mind, but it's possible. But you guys make it sound like this is always and forever, and let's face it, I just met you all. I don't know if I can get along with one of you let alone all four. And you are all so damned overprotective. Not one of you would let me ride on the back of one of your bikes."

My inner wolf whined at these words from my mate, but I had to be strong and not let him get the best of me. I didn't like hearing these words, but from a human perspective, she was correct.

I put my fingers on her chin and raised it, so my eyes met her.

"The bike thing bothered you," I said.

She bit her lip then nodded. "Nona taught me to be self-sufficient and to make my own decisions. I can't wrap my head around men telling me what I can and can't do. If that's what it's going to be it won't work."

"I understand, Vivian," I said gently.

"You do? You aren't angry with me?"

"I will never be angry with—" I almost said *my mate*, but put that aside quickly. "I will never be angry with you. I won't lie and say your words please me, but I'm a realist too. If you aren't happy, none of us will be happy. So, tell me what will do that."

"I—I don't know," she stammered. "I'm so confused. It should be a slam dunk. You are all—amazing. And I want you, all of you, and I'm having trouble accepting that. Add your bossy natures to the mix, and I'm in a real quandary."

"So, you need some time to think things over."

"Yes. No. I don't know. That's what's driving me crazy."

"Okay, Alpha decision time," I said.

"Oh?"

"Yes. None of us will share your bed until you've made a real decision about us."

"And if I want you to all go away?"

Never happening, protested my wolf. But I could imagine we'd book some job that would take us to the other side of the world, so was entirely possible we could leave her behind for stretches at a time.

"We'll go away."

"For good?"

"Why don't you think that over before you extract that kind of promise from me, Vivian? I can understand you questioning this situation. It's new for us too. But we want it to work too, so you have to get clear on what you want before we can give it to you."

She nodded her head. "Okay, but there's one thing."

"Oh?"

"I have to use the ladies, so is it possible I can do that without a wolf sniffing at my door?"

"She what!" I said.

Lucius smashed his hand down on the table, and the other patrons of the restaurant stared at Lucius.

"Listen up," he said in a low voice. "We have been crowding her. If you want her to accept us as her pack, you've got to ease up and give her space. This is a big leap for her."

No one received Lucius' words well, with Kyle crossing his arms across his chest, and Sean spearing his breakfast steak with his knife. It wasn't a moment of high maturity, but when our wolves get riled our more human reactions became muted.

No one spoke. What could anyone of us say? What did we know about relationships with shifter or human women? Our excursions with females were play, not serious relationship material. In a way, I understood very well, because my decision about this was made by a very primal part of myself that was governed by animal and not human instincts. I wasn't comfortable drilling down on this, but Vivian holding back pinged an old soft spot in me.

I had seen my family torn apart while I was a pup. The shock of it all had left my memories fuzzy. When humans found me on the side of the road, mud-smeared and in shabby clothes, I couldn't speak. It took me a year before I did.

By that time, I had gotten comfortable with the human family that fostered me. And during that year I got a good dose through the horror movies the other kids liked to watch of what humans thought about shifters. We were evil, dangerous, and violent. What did I have to prove otherwise? Nothing. All I had were the nightmares of watching my family murdered by creatures much like ourselves.

When you're a kid, you don't think about this, but somewhere along the way, I became ashamed of my shifter self. I kept him buried and never let him out. Oh, there were times when my blood pounded, and I wanted to run through the forests near my foster family's house, but I denied him and everything I was. I became as human as the next guy because humans were nowhere as evil as what I had inside me.

When Lucius spotted me with his Alpha nose, I was angry he made the shifter in me appear. I wanted to tear that Alpha's head off. Fortunately, he was the stronger one, and he showed me that being a shifter was nothing to fear.

But I always kept women at arm's length because how could I explain what I was? How did I not freak them out when I was a freak?

Some of that old shame clung to me, and now that Vivian had second thoughts it rose up and rattled in my gut. My wolf was massively unhappy not with Vivian, but with me for not asserting myself as her mate. I fought the wolf inside me again, telling him to cool off. Lucius was right, and we needed to give her time.

I was fighting a losing battle.

My scrambled eggs had long grown cold as Kyle and Sean

engaged in a heated discussion about the situation. And suddenly I flashed on the fact that Vivian had not returned from the ladies' room.

"Guys? How long does it take for a woman to use the bathroom?"

Here our lack of knowledge about the intimate lives of women reared its ugly head. From the expressions my pack mates faces, we had no clue.

Lucius' head snapped up.

"Go check it out then," he said.

Great. After giving us the lecture about giving Vivian her space he sends me to the bathroom to check up on her. This will not win points for me. Still—my concern outweighs my irritation and I rose from the table even though the scraping of the chair on the floor seemed overloud to me.

And those bastards watched me as I walked down the hallway toward the kitchen and the restrooms. I felt their eyes bore into my back as the scent of their concern wafts off them. They owed me big time, and I'd make sure I get it out of their hides.

My ears strained to hear anything through the door, the snap of tissue off its holder, water running in the sink, feet scuffling on the tile—but nothing, as if no one was in there.

I knocked on the door.

"Hey, Vivian," I said. "It's Daniel. Are you okay?"

I waited a couple of seconds, but now my concern turned to worry, and I jiggled the handle which was locked, but the bolt snaps free from the doorjamb, and the door swung open.

No Vivian.

Hell.

Worry morphed into alarm, and I twisted toward my pack who saw my reaction. Lucius hand signed to the others to check outside, and gave me the signal to follow her scent trail.

It wasn't hard. She wasn't in the bathroom long before she went out the window over the toilet. Vivian was almost petite, and her slim frame could easily fit through. I scent something else—another person, male. My wolf growled within me at the thought of another male touching my mate.

Lucius joined me outside.

"Smell that," I said.

"Yes," said Lucius tightlipped. When the danger quotient zoomed, our Alpha tapped his emotions down, radiating confidence he probably didn't feel. Kyle and Sean joined us at the back of the restaurant.

"I caught her scent at an empty parking spot," said Sean. "She was frightened."

Lucius' eyes glowed with repressed anger.

"We'll find her."

"The main route is less than fifteen minutes from here," said Kyle. "We should take the truck and check out if any suspicious vehicles are making for it."

"Go, Kyle. Keep your phone line open. The rest of us, saddle up and let's see what we can find. There's got to be some clue. I'll go check the gas station first to see if anyone saw anything."

"I'll go check the house. If it was the cartel, they want what Vivian has, and that is the first place they'll look."

"I'll go with you," said Sean who flicked the truck keys at Kyle, who tossed him the bike fob.

"Keep—" started Lucius.

"Yeah, I know. The phone line open," I said as I plugged in my Bluetooth headpiece. Sean started a group call and we all got on it. As soon as I started the engine, I headed down the road, the engine rumbling between my legs, eager to get to the house.

"Those bikes are loud," shouted Kyle in my headpiece.

He was right and half a mile from the house I pulled off,

and Sean pulled up behind me. Stealth was a no-brainer. I tossed my keys to Sean and then gave him my phone.

"Hold those," I said as I stripped.

"Hey!"

"I'll get there faster on four legs than two."

"Bastard," he muttered because I was right, but someone had to bring my clothes. I stuffed them into his hands.

"I will not clean the ticks out of your fur," he called after me.

Still, my only concern now was Vivian. He was just upset I shifted before him, leaving him with housekeeping duties.

My paws kicked up the sand at on the shoulder of the highway, spraying Sean with my commentary on his snotty words. We were resistant to disease, so ticks weren't a health concern, but they were itchy; a brother's help was a necessary evil.

I had to keep to the blacktop though, because the thick underbrush beyond the shoulder of the road prevented easy passage. The sandy shoulder could easily hide bits of glass, a discomfort I didn't need, so my paws hit the hot road double time. As I run, I thought about how that bastard Rick exposed Vivian to danger, and if I ever saw him, I would put a world of hurt on him.

Within minutes the hedgerow that bordered Vivian's property appeared on my left, and I watched for a space I could burrow through the shrubs. The bushes were old enough to have grown woody trunks where the branches shot off and mingled with neighbor boughs leaving small gaps between the ground and green. I should have paid more attention to this during my patrol, and now I kicked my ass for not doing so.

A larger spot than the others caught my eye and I squeezed under. The branches hit my nose and scrapped my back, but I pushed through because haste was needed. Vivian was in danger.

I spotted a large and unfamiliar black van in the driveway; someone wasn't being subtle so I decided I didn't need to be. I howled a long wail letting Sean know to hurry and to tell Lucius and Kyle to get here quick.

I'd found Vivian, and now I have to save her.

SEAN

If Daniel thought he was the only one with skin in the game, he was wrong. It was just like him to shift at a moment's notice when the job was on the line. I almost couldn't blame him, but I was left to run along the blacktop with cars whizzing by me holding his stinky clothes. The man needed to send out his cleaning.

The only reason I thought about this was that I didn't want to think about what may be happening to Vivian. That cartel roughed up Robbins good, and it was a miracle we made it to the hospital in time.

What would they do to her?

Robbins was an ass to stick sensitive information on her, even more so because he didn't tell her what he did. Of course, company men did what they needed to get the job done, but still, a college student? She didn't sign on for this intrigue, so Robbins better not cross my path again.

I caught Daniel's scent as I got near the hedge. He had run hard and threw off enough musk to warn every creature in the area that a predator ran near.

Daniel's howl split through the neighborhood.

"Sarg," I huffed into my headset, "Daniel found something at Vivian's house. You should get here."

"On my way," Lucius and Kyle snapped in my ear. Damn. I winced; they didn't need to speak loudly. I heard them just fine.

I waited behind the hedge, not wanting anyone to see me. I can tell you this: I didn't like it one bit. Daniel found me and lay on the ground on the other side of the hedge.

"Hey," he said.

"You shifted?"

"Just for a minute. I got a look inside the house. I couldn't see Vivian, but I smelled her."

"Dude, it's her house."

"It's a fear scent, so yeah, she's in there."

I put his clothes on the ground and started tearing at mine.

"Then we should get her."

"No, we need to wait for Lucius and Kyle. We don't know how many are in there or what weapons they have."

"Some scout you are," I said derisively as I picked up his clothes. I walked to the entrance of the driveway. The house was in the middle of the property, set off from the road and the front door pointed south instead west toward the highway. On top of that, a large oak tree grew on this side of the house blocking the windows on the side toward the road, so I understood why Daniel shifted here. No one would see him from the house.

Daniel stared at me as I took off my shoes.

"I told you."

"And I told you I'm going to get her," I said as I undid my belt. I wouldn't be holding back, not this time. All my pack's ribbing about how I faint in the face of danger prickled me now. Now it was Daniel that was unwilling to take the risk, and in my eyes, this was *not* the time to do that. "Either you come with or not."

"Lucius will have a fit."

"He can kiss my ass."

"No, more like whup it."

"Let—" I started to say, but a high pieced scream rose from the house, knifing the air with its distress. My alarm sensor ratcheted to razor sharpness. One of her captors must have silenced her, and my mouth tightened when I thought of how he might accomplish that.

"I'm going, and you can't stop me."

With that I morphed into wolf form, kicking off my pants in my first leap across the lawn. In the heat of August, the burnt-out grass prickled the space between my paws pads, and usually, that would spur me forward, but this day I needed no such inspiration. My mate was in danger, and I needed to get to her.

In our tightening of the house's security we sealed all the windows shut, so unless I broke one, which would be noisy therefore dangerous for Vivian, there was no easy access to the house. I thought about the basement window I stupidly left open. That was a security risk, but perhaps my only way into the building.

Lucius would kill me when he found out about the window—but not so badly if I saved our mate.

I let my body scrap along the side of the house as I circled it to keep whoever was inside from seeing me. Pebbles edging the foundation stuck in my paws, and I had to resist the urge to growl.

I found the window by the moldy stench that wafted from the basement. Goddess, I hated the place, and the last thing my wolf wanted was to enter that stink hole, but this was for my mate. My nose crinkled though when I stuck my muzzle through, but I had to test whether my head would fit. If it did the rest of my body could squeeze inside.

My human side prickled even at this caution, aware our mate was in the hands of those who would do her harm, while my wolf tested my capacity to follow my human plan. It was a graceless entrance, with me twisting my body to fall through the opening and a hard fall on hard packed earth that nearly drew a yelp from me.

I shook my body to recover, shedding my trepidation and the dirt of the floor at the same time. With quick, silent steps I trotted up the stairs and nuzzled the handle to find the door locked. Opening it would require human skills, and I contemplated the best way to do this. When I entered, what would happen? If they saw a beast, they'd shoot first, so even if I felled one, I might have others unloading bullets into me.

Naked man? Not so good.

Then I remembered my laundry in the dryer. For once it paid to be sloppy. I shifted at the dryer and pulled out sweats and dressed.

Now it was my bare human feet that trod the stairs to the door. Still locked, of course, and I had to think about what to do. My eyes swung through the basement, and I saw Daniel's tool box. Hopefully, in his spending spree at the hardware store, he scored something that would help me open this door.

Footsteps overhead creaked the floorboards in a repeated loop signaling a sentry. I pictured in my head where he walked in the house. The basement door fed into the kitchen, with the dining room on the far right through an arched doorway, which was adjacent to the living room's far end toward the kitchen—again accessible through another arch. He walked circuit, kitchen to dining room to living room through the hallway which housed the stairs to the second floor, to the kitchen again. There was a sitting room opposite the living room, but he didn't walk there, so most likely he just glanced inside. That would have been a good point of entry, but the tall windows were sealed shut.

If there was one sentry, there were at least two men. I could handle that.

Vivian was silent, and this only makes my wolf push me to get to her soon. If she was hurt, I would never forgive myself.

Daniel's toolkit yields a package of screwdrivers still sealed in their sealed plastic bubbles. This is the one time I praise him for his fascination with buying tools. Screwdrivers are good. The one with the long shank would be an especially good improvised weapon. With my bare hands, I ripped it apart, an impossible task for anyone but a shifter.

Weapon in hand I advanced on the door and pried the flat end between the jamb and the door, seeking the bolt. If I was lucky, I could push the bolt away from the plate that secured it in the frame.

I guide the head of the screwdriver in and find my target. With some judicious wriggling of the handle, and the pressure of the screwdriver, the bolt slipped out of the plate opening the door suddenly. With it, I fall. As I do, a sharp pain burst at the back of my head—lights out for me.

KYLE

"Where the fuck is Sean?" said Lucius as he and Kyle dropped next to me on the lawn as I stared at the house. Lucius sniffed the air seeking Sean's scent, and our Alpha's mouth formed a tight line as he deduced what I would say next.

"He went in."

"Asshole," snapped Kyle.

"Vivian screamed. He couldn't wait."

"Has she made any noises since?" Lucius stared intently at the house as if he could see more than me. He couldn't; we were all working blind here.

"Not that I've heard."

"Let's go then," said Lucius as he peeled off his shirt.

Lucius took the west side of the house, closest to where Sean disappeared. We took the east side pointing toward the river, sniffing for Sean. We ran past the front entrance, using their parked van for cover, and then around the garage. We stopped just before the back porch jutted from the back of the house, expecting a guard there. That there wasn't one was good news.

Around the porch we found Lucius sniffing at a window. He poked his head at the glass, and it swung open. He glanced at us, and we didn't have to read each other's minds. Sean entered here.

One by one we flopped to the floor because we had to twist uncomfortably to fit our bodies through the opening. Lucius was at the stairway first, and his eyes narrowed as he regarded the closed door. He padded up the steps and poked his muzzle gently at it, and the door opened a crack.

Score one for Fire Team Wolf. Sean had broken the lock. But tactically we were in a poor position. We had to travel upstairs and face an unknown number of adversaries. There was only one thing in our favor.

Surprise.

Lucius scrambled to the base of the stairs and then trotted halfway the length of the basement. With a fierce swish of his tail he turned and charged the stairs, and we followed, bursting into the kitchen.

The first one patrolling with a rifle in hand didn't have a chance. Lucius ripped out his throat before the man could raise his firearm. I could see where I would be calling our cleaning service to get this mess cleared up before law enforcement came poking around. Oh well, our profit margin got ripped to shreds with the charter plane.

Daniel tore through the dining room and then the living room to meet me at the base of the stairs. With only the first one on the first floor, whatever others—including—Vivian and Sean were on the second.

Lucius met us and glanced up the stairs, and a bedroom door creaked open.

"¿Qué está pasando allí?"

Lucius gave a wolf laugh which was a fearsome sound, a cross between a bark and a howl. In answer, a wiry man whose muscles ran in cords through his arms poked his head out of bedroom door at the top of the stairs. He raised his arm, and we all saw and smelled the gun: a semi-automatic pistol that could take all of us out in seconds. Daniel and I scattered, but Lucius stormed the stairs as shots rang out. We watched helplessly as he tumbled to the bottom of the stairs.

I shifted and pulled him back towards the kitchen. He panted heavily, and I felt around trying to find the wounds.

"Okay, pendejos," said the man in a thick Spanish accent. "I know who and what you are. I've got your woman up here. I smell all of you on her, and maybe when I get done with you, I'll take her too."

Daniel poked his head through the kitchen door and helped me pull Lucius back. He pulled my medical kit from the pantry closet where we stored it and set it down next to me while I evaluated our Alpha.

"How bad?"

Lucius changed, a prodigal stunt in his condition, and he glared at us.

"Not enough to kill me, assholes. Get Vivian. That guy is a shifter, and there's no telling what he'll do to her."

Daniel and I exchanged looks because we did not get that scent.

"You sure?"

"His scent is weird, but I got close enough to know what he is."

"Where are you hit?" I said unwilling to let my assessment go. We can't lose Lucius, not now or ever.

"He grazed my ear. That's it. Hurts like a mother."

I examined his head, where a bullet grazed the skull. If he were human, with the percussive force, he'd be out cold.

"Idiot," said Daniel. "Your thigh too."

Daniel was right. Blood oozed from Lucius' thigh, but it was a flesh wound nothing more.

"Nothing that won't heal. Get me up."

"You should rest," I protested.

"And you should shut the fuck up."

"He's the Alpha," said Daniel. Between us, we got Lucius on his feet.

"Now what?" I said.

"We'll call the bastard out."

Lucius limped to the side of the stairwell.

"Hey, pendejo," he sneered. "Get your scraggly ass down here and face me like a man."

"I've got your woman," the shifter called.

"Keep her. We'll get another."

"So," the intruder said, "she doesn't matter at all."

Vivian made noises of protest through a gag, and I peered up to see the gang member holding her neck while he held a gun to her head.

"You bore me, *pendejo,*" said Lucius. "Do what you want, and then I'll come to get you."

Vivian's eyes glowed with pure fright, and I didn't blame her. This was a dangerous game that Lucius played.

Behind the gangster, the bedroom door opened a crack. It could only be Sean, and I was right. He rushed out of the room and threw his arm around the shifter's neck breaking the man's hold on Vivian.

"Run, Vivian!" he called as the man struggled in his arms.

Several things happened at once.

Vivian practically flew down the stairs and landed in Lucius' arms.

Lucius shouted: "Watch out, Sean! He's a shifter!" He handed Vivian to Daniel, who held her tight, and spoke soothing words in her ear. That was when I saw something I never did before.

The man shifted, but not as a wolf. Instead, a snarling, humongous python twisted around Sean.

"Fuck!" shouted Lucius. He scrambled up the stairs, and I

followed, human feet morphing into paws, and we both landed on top of the twisting mass of reptile. He hissed and snapped at us as we bit him wherever we could strike. Blood spurted everywhere, smeared on the snake's scales and on Sean. I had no idea how badly Sean was injured between all the gore and the fighting. Finally, Lucius clamped his jaws on the creature's length just below his head, and it uncoiled around Sean as its body furiously convulsed. I grabbed the end of its tale, stealing some of its ability to move, while Lucius held on shaking his head back and forth. With a final gasp the light of life died in the python's eyes, and he hung limply in Lucius' mouth.

The roar of an enraged jungle cat sounded from the kitchen, and in a holy fuck moment, I remembered the guy we supposedly killed. I tore down the stairs and pushed into the kitchen to come face to face with an honest-to-god jaguar, its human clothes still hanging on its body. The thing hissed at me, backing up toward the door.

"Don't bother to come back," I said. "Or we'll do to you what we did to your friend."

I shifted, and its green eyes turned wide.

It hissed again, but went out the door and soon after I heard wheels rolling over the crushed gravel of the driveway. Daniel and Vivian came up behind me, and instinctively I put my arm around her too.

"Why did you let him go?' Daniel fumed.

"To send a message not to bother us again. If they're smart, they'll listen. If not, they know what we can do."

"Great," gasped Sean, bring up the rear leaning on Lucius. "You don't give me a chance to whup his ass. He gave me one hell of a headache."

He winced when he spoke.

"Serves you right, corporal," growled Lucius. "That's what you get for disobeying orders."

"Technically, I didn't disobey any orders."

"Technically, Sean," said Vivian, "you gave me a heart attack when they dragged you unconscious up the stairs. So, try not to do that again."

"Again?" I said.

"Well, you boys have to stick around to clean up the mess you made. Because I'm not cleaning up snake. And if you do that well, maybe you can stay a little longer."

VIVIAN

ne year and four months later
    Where the hell are they?
It was cold out here, outside my house, in the middle of the Connecticut winter. I saw the Christmas lights on the tree one of them must have set up in the living room. But I saw none of their vehicles.

I just flew in for Christmas vacation after finishing graduate school, and though they warned me that they wouldn't be meeting me at the airport, I was disappointed that at least one of them didn't show.

Rick cleared up everything with school, and they welcomed me back—mostly because Lucius came down hard on him. It was a very uncomfortable moment when Rick showed up at the house a week after the boys saved me from the cartel goons, and I think it was a closer call than Rick let on that he got out of our house alive. But he retrieved the intel he hid, in of all things, my backpack. He'd disguised it as a fake artifact, made to look like the real thing. The bastard planned all along to use me to get the information out of Colombia which is why he brought me. Lucius escorted him to the door after that, and I heard that don't-screw-with-me tone in his voice. The next day I got the call from the college.

I didn't have long with them before I went back to Colorado, though one or another seemed to show up at my off-campus apartment throughout the last three semesters. That I always seemed to have a different man on my arm every weekend kicked up some gossip, but I was at school to learn, and not worry about anything else.

Thank the Goddess, as they say, I had them around to help me have fun while I obsessed over my studies.

I just finished and defended my thesis, drawing on carvings of San Augustine, Colombia. The people who chiseled those unforgettable images into standing stones and rock cliffs and other sculptures were lost to time. Those human faces with animal fangs remind me so much of shifters that I wondered if shifters were connected to them. I didn't make my thesis about that, but at least I explored it as a side issue as I dug out the truth of those mysterious people.

I asked the boys over and over again about their jobs, but they didn't talk. I got the distinct impression they work short-handed, so at least one could *protect* me.

In the past sixteen months, I'd gotten to know each of them separately and grown to appreciate—love—each one. Sean had a geeky charm, and he introduced me to the world of video and board games. I gained a few friends from the Dungeon & Dragon games he ran when he visited.

Daniel. Such a tough guy on the outside and a total romantic on the inside. What woman can argue with that? Not me.

Wild Kyle. He took me skiing and got me hooked. While I'm home, we're going to Vermont to catch a couple of days doing that. Kyle taught me it's okay to go all out for what I want, which helped a few times this semester when I had a professor that gave me a difficult time.

Lucius. Calm, steady, reliable, and protective. He had a fit when Kyle took me skiing. When Lucius was with me, though, I felt safe. The nights he was with me, I didn't have nightmares about violent cartels, or monster shifter snakes.

And of course Sean. He was always talking about the future and made me feel like I couldn't imagine one without him, any of them for that matter.

I drummed my gloved hands on the steering wheel of my rented car to the tune of a rock and roll song on the radio. If they didn't show up soon, I was going in. It was my own house anyway.

For now.

My phone chimed a text message.

Sean: Be right there, sweetheart.

The humongous truck they bought roared onto the gravel drive, and then Kyle's Jaguar. Who'd have thought Kyle would buy such a pricey car?

"All the better to drive you with," he grinned widely when I asked.

I grabbed up the four envelopes on the seat next to me and climbed from my car.

My four men got out their vehicles and grabbed up boxes and bags, and immediately I was crushed in group bear hug full of wolf shifters.

Among the flurry of hi's and quick kisses, I got the idea that they might have missed me.

And I missed them.

"Come," said Kyle. "We have food and drink and presents for our mate."

"Yep," said Daniel. "Champagne, and some food from a great restaurant for the shore."

"And cake," said Sean.

"Are we celebrating something? A big job?"

"A big something," said Lucius mysteriously. "Though it

all depends on you. First, we want you to see what we've done while you've been away."

"What did you do?"

"Everything we could," said Kyle with a mischievous grin.

"Oh boy," I said.

"Now wait. Close your eyes."

"Here, I'll help," said Sean and he pulled my cap over my eyes.

"How am I supposed to walked up icy stairs with my eyes closed."

Lucius came up behind me. "I'll make sure you don't fall."

"Don't you always."

He rumbled approval and put his arms around my shoulders. As I walked forward, one of the guys opened the front door and a rush of warmth greeted me as I entered the house. Kyle pushed up the cap and stepped away. "Look around."

My eyes grew wide. My house looked brand new. The hardwood floors had been sanded and sealed, now shiny brightly. All the dingy wood from the wainscoting on the lower half of the walls to the molding around the doors and the rails of the stair were all a shiny white. New wallpaper covered the walls.

"Now," said Kyle. "If you don't like anything, you let us know, and we'll change it."

"It's gorgeous. But when did you get the time to do this?"

"Lucius," said Daniel, "may have let up on his slave-driving ways."

"May have?" said Lucius.

"Now wait, there is more," said Sean. They led me into the kitchen, and I stopped short. They remodeled the floor, cabinets, counter, and appliances.

"This is too much," I said. "You shouldn't have spent all this money."

"What money. Materials are a few thou," said Kyle dismissively. "It's the labor that's expensive."

"Now," said Sean. "We haven't finished the basement yet, but we've laid down a concrete floor and installed a system to keep it dry. By next summer we'll have a nice—"

"Sean," growled Lucius.

"A nice place to play video games," he finished.

"Wow, you guys did a lot of work. It's a great Christmas present."

"Wait, we aren't done yet."

Kyle led the way up the stair to my bedroom. Only double doors replaced the single one.

"Now, we took a few liberties, but your room was just so small, so we opened it by taking the next room." He flung open the door, and the first thing I see is the huge bed in the center.

"We had to have it built custom, but it should fit all of us."

"This is too much," I whispered.

"We haven't tested it out, yet," said Sean. "We were waiting for you."

"But wait, there's more."

"You guys are crazy."

"Crazy for our mate," said Lucius.

It was Daniel that led me to the room on the right-hand side of the stairs, and this one left me speechless. I stared at it, a complete nursery. Daniel slid his arms around my shoulder.

"What do you think?"

"Think? Think? Don't you think you guys should have talked to me about this?"

"We are," said Lucius. "We know you have another year of school. We aren't pushing, but want to show you we are all in."

I turned, as tears filled in my eyes and handed them the

envelopes I had carefully prepared by Nona's lawyer. I can't speak as they stared at them.

"What is this?" said Daniel in half-joking voice to cover his nervousness. "Eviction papers?"

"It does have to do with the house."

Lucius looked at his copy. "Are you sure about this Vivian?"

I nodded, never surer of anything in my life because I had all their names added to the deed.

"My home is now yours."

"That," said Sean, "is the best Christmas gift you could have given us."

"Well, except one," said Kyle. He gave me a look I've come to know well, and I squealed as I ran from the room. And they followed me into our bedroom, just like I thought my pack would.

Thank you for reading **Mated to the Pack***! Keep the steamy romance going in the next book,* **Mated to Team Shadow***!*

CLICK HERE TO DOWNLOAD IT NOW

A frantic plea for help and then suddenly, silence. My friend Surma's gone missing, and my investigation's landed me in hot water – on a yacht partying with a known criminal in St. Lucia to be more exact.

Cornered with my cover blown, my miraculous escape grew into an even more dangerous situation. I've been kidnapped by four guys running from pirates, as if that's even a thing now?

Forced to take refuge, the tables have turned. I'm not sure if they're my captors or my saviors.

There's Ryker the Chief, Gunner, his second in command, Kane the medic and Damon the comms officer, Elite Navy SEALS but that's not all they are... and the truth might be more than I can handle.

All I know is each of them wants me, and amazingly, I want all of them. There's no time for confusion however. To survive, we've got to stick together. I'm just not sure what that means.

DOWNLOAD MATED TO TEAM SHADOW

Or keep reading for a Sneak Peek!

MATED TO TEAM SHADOW

Janine

The party pitched to full swing, and the revelers were too sloppy drunk or high to pay attention to my movements. This allowed me to poke my nose in places where it did not belong. The only people I had to watch were the four ridiculously smoking hot bodyguards dressed in black from shoulder to toe stationed throughout the yacht.

But although I acted as loopy as the tanned and toned high rollers surrounding Aedan Morgan, I could pick out a path to his office. Here I hoped to find the clue to my old college roommate's fate. At the very least, I might find convincing evidence about her kidnapping and/or Morgan's nefarious deeds.

When I use the word "nefarious," it's for good reason. Interpol suspected Morgan was the kingpin of not only drug running but Caribbean piracy. This last scored high on the law enforcement's radar because a frightening surge of pirate attacks plagued Latin America and the Caribbean last year. Law enforcement recorded seventy-one pirate attacks in the area—a one hundred and sixty-three percent increase from the previous year. Morgan certainly had a piece of that.

But no one could make a case against the elusive Morgan. The pirate playing the part of an international playboy gave the bastard plenty of cover and ability to move about the cabin, figuratively. Last I saw, Morgan sat immobile on the upper deck in a half-conscious state after sucking in several lines of pearly white coke.

It must be good to be a criminal mastermind. At least he lived well enough. The yacht, surreptitiously renamed the *Lady E*, was gorgeous though only worth thirteen million dollars. Higher-end floating palaces go for thirty-eight mil and more, but I guessed beggars couldn't be choosers when you procured your watercraft through theft. Highly polished walnut panels lined the walls, and the hallway floors had the softest carpet I'd ever felt. Yeah, I must check my bank account to see if I had thirteen mil to cover the price of one of these babies.

As if.

Newsflash. Investigative journalists beginning their careers do not make big bucks.

I smoothed my gold sequined mini-dress scored at a New York designer's showroom at a deep discount. It was not an outfit I'd normally buy. The cut dipped too low and the hem too high, but it purchased me entrée into many venues that demanded a particular cache for admittance.

At once trashy and expensive, it pegged me as the type of party girl welcomed into the dens of iniquity of the rich and famous. I checked my stylish blonde bob wig, stolen from my mother's inventory, to make sure it was in place. Then I moved forward, zig-zagging through the partygoers carefully to support the illusion I was drunk. If they caught me, I needed a plausible excuse why I veered off course.

So much depended on me not getting caught.

"Où est... salle de bain?" I said in my sloppy French, to the immobile bodyguard stationed at the doorway that led to the staterooms and Morgan's office.

He stared at me with animal dispassion as if I were prey, and I shivered. His nostrils flared, but other than that, not a single muscle twitched on his classically chiseled face.

Down girl, I thought. *You are not here to play.* Though if I were, Mr. Tall, Dark and Dangerous would tick the right boxes. Chalk it up to my intrepid and impulsive nature, but I have yet to meet an inappropriate man I'm not drawn to.

Which was why I remained steadfastly single. Still, his high cheeks, his classic straight nose, square jaw, wide shoulders and ripped abs that did *not* hide behind his black sweater whispered to me, "*Come here, little darling.*"

"The head," he replied in English, "is down the hall, second door on the right."

Head. Interesting choice of words. Marines use that term for the bathroom.

"*Merci,*" I said, and then realized I announced I understood English. *Hell. I hope I haven't blown my cover.* But I reassured myself speaking more than one language was common in most parts of the world. In contrast to the United States where it was nearly a cultural crime to know more than one language.

I fake stumbled forward and then found myself thrown into the bodyguard's solid form by a bona fide impaired guest making for the same accommodation.

"Sorry," the guest slurred, and staggered past us.

"*Excuze-moi,*" I said as the delicious bodyguard caught me in his strong arms. His scent intoxicated me with an enticing mix of sandalwood and musk.

He bent to my ear and whispered, "You can cut the bullshit French. You sound like a boarding school reject."

I pushed away with more force than my supposedly drunk condition would have allowed and glared at him.

"There is no need to be insulting," I said. "Sometimes you have to lay it on thick to get into these parties."

"Oh, I'm sure you lay something," he said with a curled lip.

"*Va te faire foutre*," I snapped. But telling the man to kiss my ass didn't illicit even a twitch.

He cocked his head. "Sorry. On duty. Better run along now. The gentleman has finished." His head snapped to level his gaze on the rowdy crowd. Dismissed, I stepped away stewing at his rude treatment until I realized the bodyguard announced the man finished before he opened the door.

Arrogant son-of-a-bitch.

I passed the drunk and slid open the door. Instead of walking inside, I looked over my shoulder to check that the bodyguard had his eyes on his paper watching the crowd. I slid it shut and tiptoed down the hall and slipped in the door I'd spotted Morgan walking from earlier.

The stateroom featured a large wood desk before an immense porthole that was more a wide pane of glass than hole looking over the St. Lucia harbor. Lights from the town sparkled in the bluish light of deep evening, seeming more like a fairyland than bustling port. We were gliding toward a slip, a sure sign the evening was about to come to a close and announced my narrowing window of opportunity.

I glanced around the cabin frustrated by the pristine cleanliness of its occupant. Who would think that an international criminal had a clean fetish? I walked to the desk and rattled each drawer to find them locked tight.

Merde.

I was not without resources, just a rapidly dwindling amount of time for my investigation. I pulled the metal nail file I hid in my bra and worked the lock of the topmost long, thin, middle drawer. This is the place where many people kept sensitive information on thumb drives.

The question was whether Morgan could be counted on to be like other people, in any respect. I had to hope so because I found no other place he could hide information.

My misspent youth hassling the principal of my high school rewarded me with a click. Heart thudding, I pulled open the desk to find a leather journal and several thumb drives.

Score!

I hope.

I pried open the leather journal to find it was a ledger with words and numbers but in Spanish. Since my Spanish was as good as my French, I couldn't make heads or tails of the words. I slipped my iPhone SE from my bra, stripped of all apps and not connected to a service. Its use was strictly to take photographs, and its compact size made it easier to conceal in clothing. I worked to steady my shaking hands as I snapped sharp photos of the pages. The ship shuddered from a bump which I could only surmise was the dock.

I was officially out of time.

One more shot and I'd have captured the written pages. I slipped the phone back into my bra. In a scorching second of bravado and heedless of the danger, I scooped up the thumb drives and stuffed them in my bra, determined I would get off this vessel before Morgan discovered the drives missing.

Or so I hoped.

The cabin door rattled, and my heart nearly stopped as I shoved the desk drawer closed.

The door flew open revealing a bodyguard. Only he wasn't tall and dark. He stood delectably tall, buff, and blond.

"Who are you?" he said with his eyes narrowed.

"I'm looking for the bathroom," I said sloppily, aiming to pull off my drunk act.

His eyes narrowed because he clearly did not believe me. His nostrils flared too and surprise lit his handsome green eyes. The bodyguard touched a headset on his ear.

"Intruder in the primary's office."

He nodded and touched the headset again.

"Roger," he said.

My stomach fluttered with a thousand nervous butterflies, and as usual in dangerous conditions, I now needed to use the bathroom, but I had to hold it.

"Oh, baby," I said in a seductive voice. "I didn't mean to make any trouble. I'll just go on my way."

But Tall, Blonde and Delicious wasn't having it as he moved to the desk, and I tried to pass by him. He grabbed my arm in a viselike grip and stopped my forward motion cold.

"Wait here," he said with utter politeness as if he was a waiter offering a menu.

"I should go," I said.

"No," said a rougher voice. Another of the bodyguards stood in the door. And this one was massive. He had to turn to get his expansive shoulders into the cabin. His deep blue eyes stared into me to the divine secrets of my soul. His nostrils flared too.

What is it with these guys flaring their nostrils?

"What do we have here?" said another voice.

Morgan came up behind the bodyguard, standing straight and utterly sober in his white linen suit. The bastard had played us all. The butterflies in my stomach morphed to big nasty moths seeking escape as suspicion glittered in his cold eyes. My heart sank as I realized that he did not buy my drunk act.

"Gunner found her here," said the big guy.

Morgan sauntered past both bodyguards.

"Find something of interest?" he said with an oily voice. I imagined a snake sliding across my skin, and I shivered.

"I was looking for the bathroom," I said.

"And found my desk instead. Let's see." He slid around the desk and pulled at the middle drawer, that I'd left unlocked. It sprung open, incriminatingly. Inwardly I cringed.

"Hmm," he said. Morgan glanced at the biggest guard. "Frisk her," he said.

I looked to Morgan and to the guards and did the math. If I didn't find a way out of here, I would disappear as easily as my friend Surma.

Tall, blonde and delicious, AKA Gunner, responded to a flick of Big Guy's head and advanced on me. I shrunk against the bulkhead and desperately searched for an out. Toeing off my sandals, I scanned the distance between my position and the door. I had to hope I had surprise and speed on my side.

I curled my body then leaped to put one foot on the desk. I jumped forward to sail past the black-garbed muscle, landed and rolled. Three years of high school gymnastics paid off at odd times, like this one. I stood and sprinted into the hallway only to run into another six-foot mountain of muscle, and he stared at me in amusement as I bounced off him.

"Grab her," said Gunner.

"We don't have time for this," said Big Guy.

"Yeah, but we can't leave her behind," said Gunner.

"Are all the guests off the ship?"

"Yes, Ryker," said the guy in the hall.

"And the crew?"

"Gave them shore leave. It thrilled them."

"Where's Damon?" said Ryker.

"Here, boss," said Tall, Dark, and Dangerous, AKA Damon.

"Let's hit it then," said Ryker. "Grab her, Gunner."

"With pleasure, Ryker." Unceremoniously, Gunner threw me over his shoulder.

"Wait," said Morgan coming from the stateroom. "What's going on?"

"We're terminating our employment," said Ryker.

As he finished speaking, a sun-splitting boom rocked the ship.

Ryker

The C-4 blast thundered through the ship, and the shockwave of the timed explosions threw us against the deck. Gunner had placed the first charge at the bow of the yacht for Morgan's benefit. But damn it, that pirate was in the wrong place, courtesy of Gunner failing to man his assigned position. He should have kept Morgan cornered until the last minute.

"Fuck!" sputtered Morgan. As he tried to stand, the second explosion splayed him across the bulkhead.

"Who are you guys?" the pirate rumbled with a dangerous tone in his voice.

"No time for chit-chat. Adios."

I eyed my team. "Go! Go! Go!" I yelled. The four of us with our guest scrambled toward the ladder that would take us below deck where the auxiliary watercraft sat. That was the plan: Get in, set the charges, steal—I mean, appropriate the speedboat and watch one slime-ball go up in flames.

The woman bounced on Gunner's shoulder spitting fury and beating his shoulders.

Too damn bad. Serves Gunner right.

"Did you unleash the moorings, Kane?"

He nodded grimly, and we moved forward with uneven steps. The ship listed to the side, toward the water and away from the dock, hampering our progress. Gunner had placed the charges this way purposefully, we didn't want to damage the dock.

We crawled through the skewed hallway to the ladder that would bring us to the lowest deck where Morgan stored the yacht's powerboat. Our getaway plan required to speed-boat; we couldn't afford to put our feet on foreign soil. Without passports and involved in a dubious operation, we couldn't count on recovery. This was strictly a "disavow any knowledge" mission, meaning that until we got into international waters, we were on our own.

Damon growled beside me. His frustration rolled over him because he knew what I would say.

"No. Not here," I said.

"Why the fuck not?"

I jerked my head toward the woman Gunner slung over his shoulder.

"Not in front of the normals."

"Damn, Gunner."

Once at the ladder, show-off Damon jumped to the lower deck. He held open his hands.

"Toss her here, Gunner."

"Toss?" she squeaked.

"Sure enough, but I get her back."

Gunner pulled her off his shoulder and dropped her feet-first as she screamed. But Damon scooped her up and thrust her into my arms. One by one our boots thudded on the metal deck, while Kane and Damon raced to push the boat into the water. Fortunately, our forced rearrangement of the yacht's hull brought the water level to the power boat's keel. However, we'd have to hurry, or we wouldn't clear the rapidly sinking opening at the stern to make our getaway. The sharp and acrid smell of diesel alerted me that at least one of the fuel tanks had ruptured, making it even more imperative that we get out of Dodge.

Gunner dropped the woman in the boat, and I stayed behind to shove the craft and ensure it cleared the sinking yacht. Damon started the engine. The glub sound of the engine almost reassured me that we'd get away clean. But the yacht listed again, and only inches remained to push the boat through the opening.

"Go!" I yelled as I ran along the side pushing, determined to make the boat squeeze through at an angle. Damon steered the sleek speedboat forward and put it in gear.

"Keep going!" I yelled again, and his expression hardened because he knew he'd be leaving me behind. We worked on the buddy system to cover each other's backs. Damon was my go-to, but I made an executive decision for their safety over mine. Damon grimaced, disliking my decision, but he accelerated and piloted the boat to clear water.

The yacht groaned and listed submerging the opening in seconds while the shell of the ceiling hovered inches above my head. Gear lining the walls of the boat bay floated in the rapidly narrowing gap. The lights flickered and snuffed, casting me in darkness. I needed out before I became a casualty. I knew better than to panic, but adrenaline pumped through me.

I jumped into the water, and the ocean surrounded me, its liquid Caribbean warmth saturating my clothes, pulling me down. With hours of training and experience kept the panic at bay momentarily, but with the ship submerging fast, my heart pounded thinking this vessel could be my coffin. I swam toward where I believed the opening should be, but it alluded me. Diesel in the water clouded my vision, and my hands couldn't find the egress to the open water.

From training, I knew I could hold my breath for three

minutes, but that wouldn't be enough time to locate the opening and then reach the surface.

Either I took extreme measures, or I was toast. And it would be ironic and a shame for a Navy SEAL to drown. Not that it hadn't happened before, but I was adamant it would not be me. I'd be damned if I let Davy Jones' locker take me.

Rising into the air pocket, I took a lungful of air and started the change. The burn began along my spine and spread to my legs, rearranging them from arms and legs into the limbs of a four-legged beast. My face elongated and my eyes and ears moved to different places. I sensed an opening underwater, as my jaguar ears caught sounds that my human ears could not, and my eyes saw flashes of movement obscured to me in human form. I sucked in a deep breath and dove, letting the rumbles, pops, and pings of the power-boat lead me to open water. As a human, this would have been impossible. As my animal self, it was easier than eating a candy bar.

The shift meant I'd lost my clothes but it was a small price to pay for my life. Freed, I paddled through the water.

The rumble of the power boat's engine grew louder, so I knew Damon had stopped her and waited for me to show. I poked my head up and roared to let my team know I was nearby, then I dove and shifted back to my human form. The sea water held me in its warm embrace while my bones realigned. Once limbs had become arms and legs, and my fur receded, I broke the surface of the water and waved.

The men appeared relieved, but they should know I'd always find a way.

I swam to the boat and Kane reached his arm toward the water to help me up into the boat. The woman's eyes grew wide at my naked state and Gunner threw a towel at me which I wrapped around my waist.

"My eyes," he whined with one of his stupid jokes.

Then Kane and Damon smiled, but it was more from relief that we'd all gotten out alive.

"Boss," said Damon as he peered over his shoulder. "We have incoming."

I swiveled my head to see a St. Lucia Coast Guard cutter heading our way. But it was an aging vessel and wouldn't match the power of this demon of the seas.

We'd chosen St. Lucia for this reason, and also because politically, they didn't mind assassinating known criminals. Their campaigns painted the island as a safe haven, carefully policed, to make it more attractive to tourists. When Damon told me, I nearly woofed my beer. St. Lucia? An eye-catching little island nation whose local law enforcement commanded the naval forces? It was an extreme solution for a tiny country. Still, we did not want to be caught by them or to have to explain why United States' SEALS were in their sovereign waters.

Damon revved the engines with a roar, and the 260-horsepower engine pulled ahead, leaving the cutter and St. Lucia a brief memory in a hopefully long life.

"How did we do?" I asked. The repeated slaps of the boat on the surface of the ocean forced me to sit, which I did next to our passenger.

"The bastard got to the dock," said Kane grimly.

"We shot. We didn't score," opined Gunner sourly. "What's Plan B?"

I needed to chew out the entire team, especially Gunner, but I was aware our guest barely clung to the bench as she shivered. She'd put up a brave front so far, but people handled stress in different ways. The last thing she needed was a Marine Sargent yelling at her.

"Alpha-Mike-Foxtrot. Time to disavow all of you and head to a nice island off the south of France."

"No can do, boss man, you can't adios us until the objective is achieved."

"How about we get our passenger to safety then and not spill mission objectives in front of civilians?"

"You've," she said, "failed in that."

I stared at her and couldn't pull my gaze away. Her eyes were the color of both sand and sea, two of my very favorite things, and her hair—wait. It glinted artificially in the sun, and something about the way it smelled confused me.

I yanked the wig off her head.

"Hey!"

Yeah, I got it now. Another woman's scent clung to the wig. I tossed it into the water.

"That belonged to my mother."

"Then why was it on your head?"

"None of your business," she snapped.

"Get her phone," said Gunner, "and the jump drives she stuffed in her bra."

"How do you—" she said indignantly.

"Sweetie, you were bouncing on my shoulder. I felt them."

"Oh, a regular princess and the pea," she snapped.

Damon chuckled over his shoulder, and Kane joined him. "That's a good name for you, Gunner. I like it," said Damon. "Princess."

"Don't you fucking dare, Darkman."

"You gonna make me?"

"Boy, boys," I said with my best authoritative air. "Let's not scare the lady with your juvenile antics."

"By all means," she said. "Let's frighten me with kidnapping and talk of assassination." She crossed her arms and stared at me as if she'd like to take a bite out of me.

Which isn't a bad idea.

I was surprised. My beast-self, my jaguar, rarely voiced

things in words. He communicated more often with a random thought or a picture that flashed through my brain. Not that he wasn't smart. However this part of me perceived the world in a more animalistic, and instinct-driven frame of mind.

Down, boy, I thought, though I knew damned well it wouldn't listen to my more human self. It never did.

I could almost hear a derogatory chuff, but I didn't have time for jaguar games.

"How soon before we meet our pickup?" I said.

"Thirty minutes, boss. At least we're on schedule."

That didn't do us a damn bit of good given we'd muffed the mission.

"Okay, go below deck and find a pair of shorts on this tub."

"Sure, boss," smirked Kane.

"And Gunner, turn your head."

"Why?"

"Just do it."

He turned his head to the sea, and I pounced on our passenger. I yanked the straps of her dress down and fished the phone and jump drives from her bra.

"What the hell?" she yelled. "Get away from me." She squirmed seeking escape, but in a boat bouncing on the surface of the sea, there were few places to go.

"Sorry, ma'am, but you can't keep pieces of evidence."

"Who the fuck are you," she snapped, "to be fishing around in my bra?"

"For today—the United States Government. That's all I can say about the matter."

Gunner

When Jeanine screamed, I wanted to grab Ryker and throw the fucker off the boat.

He was our team leader and a damned good one. Ryker saved our raggedy asses more than once, but I disliked him pawing the poor woman who had no choice in traveling with us.

"Hey!" I said.

"Stand down, Gunner," warned Ryker.

One did not mess with the Chief, but the look of shock and fright on our rescue's face clenched my gut. The need to protect her overwhelmed me, and if that meant going against my teammates and closest buddies, I would.

"You know, you could have asked before you manhandled her."

Ryker's eyes flew open at my insubordinate words. *But hell, he was out of line.*

I knelt before Jeanine because I wanted to get eye level with her, and you can't stand on a smallish boat clipping the water at high speed.

"Don't mind him. He's forgotten what women look like."

"Gunner," growled Ryker in warning. But I ignored him.

"What's your name?"

"Jeanine Lee."

"Okay, Jeanine. We will meet up with Coast Guard cutter soon, and it will take us back to the U.S., probably Miami. Is that right, Ryker?"

"Yeah. Miami," Ryker grunted.

"Then you can go where you want."

"Easy for you to say. I've locked my credit cards, ID, and passport in my hotel room in St. Lucia."

"Damon will arrange transportation to your home base. He's our logistics man."

Damon raised his hand. "Here."

"Yeah. We're acquainted. He told me I spoke shitty French."

I glanced at Damon, who, courtesy of his shifter hearing, easily caught her words over the roar of the boat engine. He shrugged his shoulders.

"Mr. Charm has his own way with women," I said.

"All of us do," Kane joked, as he climbed back on deck and handed Ryker his backpack.

"Now," groused Ryker, as he slipped the pack on, "if we'd worked this efficiently on the yacht—"

Damon shifted the boat into a faster gear making us all stumble on the deck. He wasn't in the mood for Ryker's complaints, because we all knew the plan had a high probability of failure. There were too many moving parts and too few of us, and the only one surprised it went into a ditch was our team leader.

We'd put our all into it, but sometimes, despite your best efforts, the op blew apart.

Doesn't mean we won't try again.

Kane's eyes nearly popped when he saw Jeanine's top pulled down. She wore a bra, but it was a very sexy black lace, and the way Jeanine glared was hot too.

And I liked her much better as a brunette.

"Here," he said, offering another backpack to her. "We have extra clothes in there. Cover your body."

"Why?" she snapped.

"Because we are near the equator and your fair skin will burn redder than a boiled lobster by the time we meet the cutter."

"Oh," she said. Her indignation deflated, and her shoulders drooped. She had been up all night, and her drawn eyes revealed her exhaustion. The morning sun glittered in her tired eyes as dawn broke on the ocean.

"Do we have food?" I asked.

"Here," Ryker responded, pulling out a package of beef jerky from his backpack. He held it out to me.

"Not me. Her. And water too."

And that wasn't a smart move on my part because Ryker's eyes glowed before he offered her the jerky and the water. My jaguar growled inside me disliking the predator's gaze Ryker gave her.

Mine, said my beast.

For the record, I was not a one-woman man. As jaguar shifters, our beasts were normally solitary creatures. We took our pleasures as they came, and I had no problem with that. Traveling the world like we did from one dangerous assignment to another didn't leave lots of room or time for a committed relationship.

But the woman ticked all my boxes. She was spunky, adventurous, fit, and smart. It took a special woman to keep up with me since jaguar shifters were energetic creatures.

Jeanine shivered, so I took the backpack and fished out a gray hoodie. It was a shame to cover her sexy dress, but I hated to see her in distress.

"Here you go."

She pulled it from my hand and slipped it on. I watched her every move. Her fingers and wrists bent in the most graceful way I'd ever seen, and I was fascinated. She'd painted her nails in sparkly gold to match her dress.

"Gunner," snapped Kane standing behind me. "Find something else to do besides staring."

My jaguar growled within me again, and I whipped around to face Kane. I stepped toe-to-toe to him, using my natural feline sense of balance to keep me upright.

"Mind your own business, Doc."

"Maybe it is my business."

"Knock it off you two," said Ryker with his voice low. "Sit down, shut—"

But the boat engine stuttered, and the vessel jolted us with a lurch and then stilled in the water.

"What the hell. Damon?" said Ryker. "What happened?"

"Don't know."

"I'm on it," said Kane. "Raise the engine hatch."

Damon hit the switch to lift the engine hatch at the stern, and the back seat rose to reveal the engine.

"Yep," I said. "It's an engine."

"Smart ass," muttered Kane.

"What do you think you'll do?" said Jeanine. "We're in the middle of the ocean."

"Astute observation. Check the fuel line, the spark plugs, see if I can find a simple fix."

"We call him Doc," I said, "and not just because he's our medic."

"Yeah," said Kane wriggling his hands with a smile. "I'm the man with the hands."

"Stop jawing and get going," said Ryker. "We need to make tracks."

"Can't you just call the cutter to retrieve us?"

"Sure," said Ryker. "If we want to give Morgan a clue where we are. Why do you think he's such a successful pirate? He has a bunch of ships in these waters searching for easy pickings. They are listening for SOSs, sat phone GPS signals, anything that will give them the ship's location."

Her eyes widened, but she asked a question I did not expect.

"How many ships?"

"Three, we think?"

"Have you been watching them for long?"

"What the hell? What's with the questions? And why were you in Morgan's cabin anyway going through his desk? Who the hell are you?"

"No one," she mumbled. Jeanine put on the hoodie as she

stared out over the water. And her scent shifted too, with a subtle note of fear, like she's lying.

Ryker's eyes narrowed with suspicion too.

"Gunner," said Kane. "Make yourself useful and find me some tools. They stowed none by the engine."

I looked in the storage sections under the seats, and Damon went below deck to the tiny sleeping space.

"Nothing there," said Damon.

"I've got nothing," I said. There was a length of rope, a blanket, a flare gun, and a first aid kit, and a bottle of whiskey. But no tools.

"Oh for heaven's sake," huffed Jeanine. She fished in her bra and pulled out a metal nail file. "Try this."

Kane smiled with appreciation as he took the thin piece of metal. "A gal after my heart. You know how to improvise, don't you?"

She crossed her arms and settled back in her seat.

"Anything to get us moving," she said.

"Shut your mouth and work," said Ryker. "And you, Gunner, survey the resources."

"Done." I reported the list of what I found and Ryker's expression turned sour.

"Doc, get on that engine."

"For heaven's sake," said Jeanine. "Are you always this grumpy?"

I had to turn away, so he didn't see me laughing. Chief's bad moods when an op didn't go as planned were legendary.

"Chief," said Damon, "is always this grumpy."

"Damon, give Doc a hand," growled Ryker. "We can't sit out here without power."

"Aye, aye, Chief."

"What are you guys anyway?" Jeanine said.

"That's on a need-to-know basis," grumbled Ryker.

"Since I'm on a ship in the middle of the Caribbean with

four strangers, I need to know."

Ryker raised an eyebrow and turned away.

"I'll check things down below," he said.

The Chief could be a dick, but it didn't bother us because we gave it right back. But we couldn't in front of the civilian. Her adorable face was now marred by a frustrated frown. So I sat next to her.

"Don't mind him. We let Morgan escape off that ship. It upsets him when an op gets blown."

"Let me get this straight. A mysterious U.S. government four-man team was on a ship of a suspected pirate to kill him? And screwed the op?"

"What were you doing on there? And don't tell me 'to party' because you enter a pirate's private room for only two reasons—to have sex with him, or to steal from him. Which was it?"

"I've got nothing to hide," she said lifting her chin. "A friend of mine partied with Morgan and then disappeared. She sent me a message saying she was in trouble, and then her messages stopped."

"Did you contact the authorities?"

"Which authorities would that be? Who takes an interest in a girl who parties with a suspected criminal?"

I had to admit she a point.

"What's her name?"

"Surma Jones. Black girl, 5'8", about one-hundred-fifty pounds."

"We've been on Morgan's ship for three months. I didn't see her."

She bit her lip, which my inner beast found adorable. He growled within me to get closer, and though in the back of my head I realized I shouldn't, I put my arm around her. Her hair's scent, laden with the sea, and the essence of her wafted up my nose. It was enticing and intoxicating.

Mine, said my jaguar.

Yeah, sure, buddy. And what would we do with her?

Do I have to spell it out?

The urge to nuzzle her neck came over me, and I stopped short of leaning over to put my mouth on her creamy skin. Inside my beastly side complained loudly.

Work, not play.

It was weird scolding yourself, and things got more ridiculous when my manhood stirred. But me making a play for her in front of the team wouldn't work, especially since we were dead in the water and miles from rescue.

"What are you doing there, Gunner?"

Damon looked over his shoulder, and his eyes narrowed. He appeared ticked off.

"I'm being nice."

Jeanine huffed, and I watched her nostrils flare with an unaccustomed level of interest.

"Be nice to her and leave her alone," said Damon.

"Stop your jawing, both of you." Gunner poked an oil-streaked face from the engine compartment. "I don't know. It could be a clogged fuel line. Do we have any wire?"

"There's the snare wire in the survival kit," I said.

"No," he said. "It's too thin. But, damn it, get that kit."

Jeanine huffed. "Do I have to give you every tool?" She fiddled with the clasp of her bra and pulled it through the sleeve of her hoodie. How do women do that? But I didn't understand until she pulled at the stitches of her bra and pulled out an underwire.

"There," she said holding out the curved wire. "If that doesn't work, I'll have destroyed a hundred-dollar bra for nothing."

DOWNLOAD MATED TO TEAM SHADOW

Warlock's Claim

Historical Paranormal Romance

Secrets of Storyville

A Countess Betrayed

A Harlot Betrothed

Epic World Building Academy Romance

The Broken Academy

Power of Fire

Power of Magic

Power of Blood

Pacts & Promises

Bonds

Reverse Harem Escapes – Great for a Quick Roll in the Hay with None of the Guilt

Fated Shifter Mates

Mated to the Pack

Mated to Team Shadow

Mated to the Pride

Taming Her Bears

Mated to the Clan

Protected by the Pack

Claimed by the Pack

The Descendants :

Desired by Four

Fate of Three

Shared by the Four